UNLEASHED VALKYRIE

STACY CLAFLIN

UNLEASHED VALKYRIE
VALHALLA'S CURSE - BOOK FIVE
by Stacy Claflin
http://www.stacyclaflin.com

Receive free books from the author:
http://stacyclaflin.com/newsletter/

CHAPTER ONE

I hesitate at the edge of the woods. The darkness in front of me is all-consuming. Wails sound behind me from one of the torture yards. Creepier noises come from Valhalla's forest.

My father turns around, barely visible just ahead of me. "Come on."

I have to be the rarest valkyrie of all. Not only have I married a mesmer and had a secret hybrid baby with him, but now I've met both of my parents and I'm following my father into the woods everyone fears.

All I want is to return to earth and be with my husband and baby.

"Come on," he repeats.

I take a deep breath and step between the trees. Strange creatures make unnerving noises.

"Hurry!"

I catch up with him, still not sure I'm making the right decision. "I need to return the soul of my target to the leaders. That's why I'm here."

"There isn't time for that."

Clearly. "What's going on? Did the civil war break out already?"

"You could say that."

"What am I supposed to do with this soul?"

"Hang onto it for now."

Sure, no problem. It's just the soul of a horrific murderer. Who wouldn't want to keep that?

I follow my father down the path. It's barely visible now that my eyes have adjusted. We weave around trees. The animal sounds grow louder, some high-pitched and others so low I can feel it.

"Where are you taking me?" Just because he provided half my DNA doesn't mean I trust him. He's someone I just met. A stranger who looks a lot like me.

"It isn't much farther."

"That's not what I asked."

"It's all I'm saying right now."

Figures. "Is your name Roan?"

He stops in his tracks, and I nearly crash into him. "How did you know that?"

"When I was in Australia, I overheard hunters talking about a male valkyrie in the area named Roan. It wasn't too hard to put two and two together."

"I was trying to keep an eye on you. You're too much like Astrid and me—doing things that could get you killed here."

I arch a brow, though it's doubtful he can see it. "You mean like marrying another valkyrie before retirement?"

"Precisely. However, you took it to a whole new level."

"Why have you never reached out to me? You say you were keeping an eye on me, and Mother mentioned you two have been doing that my whole life."

He sighs. "Prior to all this, I'd say keeping tabs on you would be more accurate. We *wanted* to be involved in your life more than anything. But the leaders wouldn't have anything to do with it. We were barely allowed to see you after you were born."

"Why didn't you try to hide me? Raise me quietly and in secret —like your marriage?"

"That didn't happen until later. Much later. Look, I'd be happy to answer all of your questions, but we're going to be late."

"Late? For what?"

"Just follow me."

"Fine." What other choice do I have, in the middle of these woods I've never before stepped into? I couldn't get out easily on my own, and even if I did, I have no idea what's going on inside the castle or the city with the civil war breaking out.

I only hope that by trusting my father, I'll quickly be able to return home to my husband and baby. The whole thing still feels surreal. I'd just learned I was expecting, then almost immediately had my son.

"How long was Mother pregnant with me?"

"Why are you asking all these questions now?" He doesn't slow down.

"Maybe because I've been married less than a month and we already have a baby. It was all rather sudden, and it's not a topic valkyries bring up often. I have a lot of questions."

"Understandable, but really, we have more pressing matters."

"How long?"

"Astrid doesn't stop when she wants something, either." He takes a deep breath. "I think the pregnancy lasted a month or two."

"You *think*?"

"It was several thousand years ago. A lot has happened since then. It's nothing personal."

Nothing is ever personal between valkyries.

I continue following him. I'd be better off waiting to ask my mother these questions, anyway. She'd be more likely to remember how long she'd carried a baby.

As we continue weaving our way around trees and moving in

the opposite direction of every inhuman sound, I keep my mind focused on Titan and Alaska, the baby with a name as unique as he is. It was unintentional, but because of his name, the valkyrie hunters are now searching for me in the northernmost US state. At least that should keep them away from my son, who they will want dead as much as any other valkyrie.

Valhalla will want him dead if they find out about him too.

My stomach clenches. Lurches. The thought of anyone doing anything to that sweet, innocent baby sends a surge of every possible emotion raging through me.

"Relax." He turns back and looks at me without slowing his pace. "I can feel your anxiety."

"Your grandson's life is on the line."

"Our entire species is in danger of extinction at this point."

I bite back a comment about how Alaska's life should mean more than others. "Are we almost there?"

"Close."

My body aches for Alaska. I can't help but wonder if my mother felt this way after I was snatched away from her at the rulers' command.

"Just up ahead."

I narrow my focus. I can see a light orange glow not far away. Looks like a small fire. Hushed conversation sounds from that direction.

When my father pushes away some prickly bushes and we come to a clearing, my heart pounds like a jackhammer at the sight.

CHAPTER TWO

itan

I peek out the blinds. The two valkyrie hunters are still whispering across the street. They keep glancing over at our house.

They're waiting for Soleil's return, even though the now-dead hunters told them to look for Soleil in Alaska. They'd sent word when they heard her tell me to go to Alaska, not realizing she meant for me to go to our baby. And I need to get to him, but I'm stuck in Australia for the moment.

I lower the blind and gather some things into a backpack. Mostly things I'll need while living in hiding with Alaska. I bring some of Soleil's shirts, hoping those will smell like her and bring our baby comfort.

Once I'm packed, I glance outside again. This time, there are two more hunters. At least, I assume they're hunters. It's not like the valkyrie hunters have flashing signs announcing themselves.

I pull out my phone and text Eveline. *Where are you?*

Sorry. Got held up. Almost there.

There are a group of hunters gathered outside.

Is Soleil back?

No. But I want to get outta here.

She doesn't respond, so I look outside again. Still four of them, but one is on the phone. Calling another four, I imagine.

Crash!

I drop the blind and turn toward the living room.

Eveline appears through a portal and turns to me. "Ready?"

"Let's go." I want to ask if she has a rune to travel to the dragon city, but I don't dare speak it aloud. What if the hunters can hear me?

A shiver runs down my spine at the thought.

I hurry over to the witch and place my hands on her shoulders so we can travel through the mirror to the Pacific Northwest.

"Close your eyes."

"Right." I close them, and before I know it, a dizzying feeling sweeps over me. Once my feet touch another floor, I open my eyes.

We're in my and Soleil's room at the dragon castle. Relief floods me as I see Fox and Calla sitting on the sofa with my son.

I rush over to them. "Thank you for taking care of him. He's been taking the dragon formula?"

"Like a champ." Calla gives me a reassuring smile as she hands Alaska to me.

I cling to him and take in his sweet aroma.

"Have you heard from Soleil?" Calla stretches.

"Not yet. The good news is she killed her target. She could be negotiating her retirement as we speak."

Fox puts his arm around Calla and smiles. "Wouldn't it be great if she gets it?"

"I'm not going to hold my breath. Not with the civil war."

"You never know." Calla gives me a hopeful look.

I shake my head. "I do. It's Valhalla's leaders we're dealing with. They don't care about anything other than their own agenda. Soleil's a soldier, and that's all they see. She's not supposed to have emotions or hopes or any of that. Definitely not love or a family."

Calla and Fox both frown.

I sit on the bed and look at my sleeping baby. He's like an angel—actually, he *is* an angel. Half angel of death and half trickster.

Marked for death by ancient rules.

I hold him a little tighter. His eyes flutter, and his mouth suckles like there's no reason to have a care in the world. I'll do whatever I can to make sure he continues to feel that way for as long as possible.

"When do you think she'll return?" Calla asks.

I frown. "No idea. Not soon enough—that's all I know. Never is, when they snatch her away."

Calla nods.

Knock, knock!

Before I can respond, the door opens. Expecting our too-young servant, I'm surprised when a burly guy marches in. He's enormous. Towers over Fox, who isn't small by any means. Could eat me for a snack then bench press a bus without breaking a sweat.

"Who are you?" I keep my tone light, like he doesn't intimidate me.

The dude barely glances my way. "The bodyguard assigned to the baby." His voice is even deeper than I expected. "Anyone tries to hurt or take him, I kill them."

That does offer me some comfort. "I'm his dad," I say quickly.

He nods then leans against the wall. "Pretend I'm not here."

Right. That'll be no problem. He's as big as an elephant, and I'm supposed to forget he's in the room.

Fox yawns. "You want us to stay here?"

"You guys can go to your room or back home. I'm staying with Alaska until I hear from Soleil."

Calla rubs her eyes. "We've been up with him for a while. A nap would be great."

"We're just next door." Fox nods in the direction. "Let us know if you need anything."

I glance at Burly. "I'm sure we'll be fine. Thanks so much for staying with Alaska."

Calla smiles. "We're glad to help. I hope Soleil returns quickly."

We say goodbye, then they leave. Burly doesn't budge as they walk past.

"You don't have to stand," I offer.

"Forget I'm here."

"Sure, whatever. I'm going to sleep too."

He nods.

"I'm going to undress."

The guy doesn't move.

"Okay, then." I lay Alaska in the middle of the bed and kick off my shoes.

Burly keeps his focus on a bare wall.

I watch him for a moment, then change inside the enormous closet. I'm pretty sure it's bigger than the house we're renting in Australia.

Then I climb into the bed and pull my son close. My heart aches for Soleil. It's hard not to imagine the worst. Not when she's broken so many of Valhalla's rules. Technically she'd been skirting them before, but now she's an all-out rebel.

I play with my wedding ring as I replay our wedding in my mind. Thinking of happier times is the only way I'll manage any sleep before Alaska wakes. If I picture her in the torture yards, I'll just fret and worry. She returned with her target's soul. Hopefully that'll be good enough for them, and they'll send her back.

At this point, I don't care if they give her another target. I just want her back with us.

CHAPTER THREE

oleil

"Come on," my father urges.

In front of me, circling around a fire, sit the three judges, Sessa, Ellika, and about fifty others.

I turn to my father. "I need to know what's going on."

"You know about the opposition. Astrid said she filled you in."

"Sessa and Ellika—"

"Are on the right side. They got bad information about your mother and me. Everyone here is trustworthy."

My heart thunders, but I stand steady. "Against all of Valhalla?"

"This is the core group of leaders."

"Whoa! Hold the phone. Why am I here?"

"Because we all agree you're one of us."

My mind spins. "I don't want this. Send me back."

"I don't have those powers."

"The judges do. Let me give them my target's soul so they can send me home. I want my retirement."

He frowns. "Nobody's retiring now. Not until this is over."

My breath hitches. "Is it true? Those in retirement are being called back into service?"

"Correct. Let's go. They're all waiting for us."

I take a deep breath. "What other choice do I have?"

"That's the spirit." He places a hand on my shoulder, and we walk over to the group. We sit near some valkyries I've never seen.

I look around the group, trying to figure out how many I know. There are more I recognize but can't think of their names or when I met them before. My father is the only male in the group, and I don't see my mother.

The shortest judge stands and puts her hands up. "Now that we're all finally here, we can begin. I want to clarify some rumors before we start. It's true that Odin and the other top leaders haven't been seen in some time. How long is up for debate and really isn't important. It's been more than long enough. Things are falling apart at the top leadership levels below them, as evidenced by the number of high officials here tonight."

I glance around again, trying to place the leaders, but can't.

Hopefully this isn't a trap. I don't trust valkyries—my parents included, at this point. And Sessa and Ellika have some serious explaining to do when I can get them alone.

The judge continues speaking. "Everything is a mess in the city, and things are falling apart on Earth. Reports of hunters are increasing daily. More human destruction and natural disasters have been happening. Targets are acting ahead of schedule, inflicting large-scale damage. It's only going to get worse until we fix it all."

My stomach clenches. Will Alaska forget about me before I can return to him and Titan?

Several people call out questions—things I'm already wondering.

"How will we get the numbers we need?"

"Do we have a chance at defeating the leaders?"

"What's the plan?"

"Who else are we going to recruit?"

The judge holds up her hands again. "I know we all have questions. So do I. In the current state of affairs, yes, it's possible for us to win. Changes have been brewing for hundreds of years. Most of you are unhappy with the way things are run, at least on some level. The requests for retirement have been off the charts as of late. We need to find all the disgruntled, unhappy valkyries we can and get them to join us. It's high time for a democracy and for our people to have a say in the laws that rule our lives. Who's with me?"

Everyone raises a hand and shouts an affirmation. Everyone but me. My head is spinning and I don't react.

Then the judge looks directly at me. "Who's with me?"

What other choice do I have? I join the others and raise my hand while calling out my agreement.

I'm officially part of the opposition. I've picked my side, and there's no going back.

Once everything quiets down, the judge speaks again, giving instructions on what needs to be done, both in Valhalla and on the Earth. "Most of you will need to stay here and help recruit from both the castle and city with us. However, we do need some to return to Earth, not only to recruit the valkyries down there, but also to gather against the hunters."

My hand shoots up in the air before I have a chance to think about it.

The judge stares at me. "Are you volunteering to lead the movement on Earth?"

My heart skips a beat, but if that's what it'll take for me to head back to my family, I'm in. "Yes."

She glances at my father. "Will you return with her?"

I turn to him, pleading with my eyes and trying to send a telepathic message to say yes.

He nods. "Astrid and I have already gathered a small but mighty group in El Salvador where there's an unusually large concentration of hunters."

"Very good. You take her, Sessa, and Ellika to Earth. The rest of us will focus on the mess up here."

My pulse drums in my ears. Sessa and Ellika. The last valkyries I want to deal with because they gave me their targets then lied to me about my parents being dead. But if I get to return home, there isn't much room for me to complain. Plus, going to Earth will give me all the time and space I need to get the truth out of them. They owe me that much.

The judge gives instructions, but I can barely concentrate. I just want to get back to Titan and Alaska. Nothing else matters.

"Time to go." My father pats my arm, and I realize the others are waiting for me. Sessa and Ellika are standing with one of the judges.

"Right." I rise. "Just trying to make sense of everything."

"It'll all make sense, I promise." We walk over to the others.

The judge makes eye contact with each of us. "You'll need to check in regularly." She looks at me. "With you being in charge, we'll send for you to give us reports as needed."

I force a smile. "Wonderful. So glad I volunteered."

She nods, clearly oblivious to my sarcasm. "If any of you need to contact us, simply take out someone with your sword. Things are so haywire up here, I'm not sure a sword-kill will bring you here. I'm going to send someone in to make sure the system is acting up even more."

"And you're sure nobody suspects you?" I ask.

"Correct. The three of us have a group of valkyries working for us around the clock to protect the cause. Nobody above us has reason to suspect a thing—not that they have time to worry about the likes of us." She looks at me. "Hand over your target's soul."

I reach for the soul and hand it to her, cupping my palms around it.

She takes it, then meets our gazes again. "Now I'm going to send you back, so we can take the others back to the castle."

I close my eyes and hope for the best. When I open them, the four of us—my father, Ellika, Sessa, and me—are standing on sand with blue-green water lapping near our feet. It's blindingly bright after being in the dark Valhalla forest.

Half-squinting, I glare at Sessa and Ellika. "Care to explain yourselves now?"

Sessa glances at my father before looking at me. "Like Astrid told you, we're on your side."

"Why'd you tell me my parents were dead?"

"Again, like you've already heard, we were given bad information. We never intended to mislead you."

Ellika steps closer, pleading with her eyes. "She's telling the truth. Honestly, Soleil. I would never do anything to deceive you."

I take a deep breath. "I want to trust you, but you two took off after I killed both of your targets. That left me with my own. I've killed four targets in the span of a few months! I didn't even get credit for half of them."

My father places a hand on my shoulder. "If you get your retirement, then it'll be worth it. We need to focus on the future, not the past."

I turn to him, struggling to keep my emotions in check. "If I'm going to lead this massive mission, I need to know I can trust everyone on our team."

"What can we do to prove ourselves?" Ellika asks.

I give her a double-take and then frown. "I'm not sure. You have to admit it was all a huge blow—you may as well have stuck your sword through my heart."

She nods. "I can see how you'd feel that way. Would you like to give us your current target?"

I start to say yes, but then realize the judges didn't give me another. I'm on Earth without a target!

My father looks at me. "If you have any trust in me, then let me take responsibility for these two. Astrid and I will work with them closely."

I take a deep breath and consider it, nearly ready to agree just so I can leave the beach and see my family. But then I make eye contact with both Sessa and Ellika. "Why did the judges send me on a mission to find you? It doesn't make any sense."

They glance at each other before Sessa speaks. "It was a test. You passed, clearly. Now you're our superior."

My father chuckles. "And mine. I get the feeling you want to get back to your family—"

I nod.

"The three of us will join your mother in El Salvador and fill in the other valkyries on the meeting back there in Valhalla. We'll be in touch. You'll need to look into the hunter situation."

"Sure thing. They already seem to be especially interested in me."

"Sounds good. We'll be in touch soon. Very soon."

"Perfect." I close my eyes and think of Titan and Alaska, ready to teleport.

CHAPTER FOUR

itan

I place a block on the tower, then Alaska reaches for it with his chubby hands and knocks the whole thing over. He bursts into a fit of laughter and pulls on a sandy-blond curl. I laugh but I can't ignore the worry and heartache that never leave me.

Soleil has been gone four months now. Each day that passes makes me worry all the more that she'll never return. I try not to picture her in the torture yards. Not to imagine her in agony, paying for the crime of marrying me and having a hybrid baby.

Alaska grunts as he tries to replicate the tower I built. His thick little fingers make it almost impossible. I smile at him as I start the new tower for him.

Knock, knock!

I open my mouth but before I make a sound, Alaska's dragon bodyguard speaks. "Enter!"

Will I ever get used to him? He picks a new spot in our room each day and stands in place, not looking directly at us. Then when we leave the room, he follows discreetly behind us. Always there but never wanting me to acknowledge him.

Iris, the young servant, enters with a platter of food.

Alaska squeals. Now that he's allowed a little real food, he associates her with the dragon delicacies.

It kills me that Soleil isn't here for all these firsts. She missed the first time he rolled over and sat up by himself. Missed his first laugh and first bite of food.

How many more firsts will she miss out on?

I've been showing Alaska pictures of her constantly. Talking about her. I'm not sure if any of it is sinking in—How much can a baby understand?—but I won't stop until she's as real to him as I am. It's impossible, and I know it. He needs to be in her arms, to hear her voice, to feel her love.

And I hate Valhalla for taking that from us.

Iris sets the trays on the table then turns to me with a slight bow. "Do you need anything else?"

Just to have Soleil back.

I shake my head. "No. Thank you."

"Let me know if you think of something." She bows again then leaves.

Alaska reaches for the table.

My stomach growls, but I don't care. With Soleil gone, I barely eat—just enough to keep myself going for our son.

I pick him up and take him to the table.

A flash of light blinds me. I close my eyes and cover Alaska's.

"Titan!"

Soleil's voice.

I open my eyes and crazy, wild emotions run throughout. She looks exactly as she did when she was taken to Valhalla months ago. Same clothes, same smear of makeup on her eyes. It's like the months she was gone never happened. Except for—

"Is that Alaska?" Her eyes widen. "He's gotten so big!"

Before I have a chance to respond, she has her arms around us both.

"Mama!"

My breath hitches. His first word, and Soleil's here for it!

He reaches for her then clings to her.

Happy tears sting my eyes. Alaska hasn't forgotten her.

The three of us hug and exchange kisses before sitting at the table. Still holding Alaska, she takes the lid off the closest tray. "I'm starving."

Alaska reaches for the piece of chicken she grabs.

She kisses his hand. "Only milk for you."

I give him a small piece of an avocado. "Actually, he's eating some food now."

Soleil freezes. "Now? Don't tell me time passed differently again?"

The pained look in her eyes guts me. "Four months. You've been gone four months."

Her mouth gapes. "I was hoping he was just growing rapidly like he did in the womb."

I shake my head. "His growth seems on point—at least for mesmers. I'm not sure about valkyries."

She holds him closer and breathes in his full head of hair. "But he remembers me."

"I made sure of that. He has every picture of you on my phone memorized. I've told him all about you."

She mutters something about making Valhalla pay.

"How long do you get to stay?" I ask. "What happened in the four months you were gone?"

"It didn't feel that long for me. Probably because of the woods. Time probably passes even faster in there."

"Huh?"

Soleil shakes her head. "Never mind. I should be able to stay here for a while."

"What's a while, and why do I sense a 'but' coming?"

"Things are out of control up there. Valkyries are piling in like I've never seen, and it's been confirmed that Odin and the others are missing. The civil war is officially on, and I'm leading the coup here on earth."

My mind spins with new information. "You're leading a coup?"

"The good news is that if we win, I'll be free. Being an agent will be completely voluntary."

"I like the sound of that, but if your side loses?"

Her expression contorts. "Let's just hope that doesn't happen."

The words shred my heart. "Don't try to protect me."

"Right. I'll be sent to the torture yards for treason."

I swallow. "For how long?"

She plays with a lock of Alaska's hair. "Eternity."

"Can you hide? Stay here in the dragon city? Only dragons can enter through the door."

"*I* just got in."

I open my mouth to respond, but then close it. Clearly, it is possible for valkyries to get in. "So, you aren't safe even here?"

"I am, at least for now. But I can't stay here. I'm leading the opposition on earth. Hiding isn't possible."

"How did this happen?" I rub my temples. "You went from staying off their radar for ten years every time to this."

"Believe me, this is far from what I want—especially the timing —but Valhalla is falling apart. They're calling in valkyries from retirement, and making everyone choose a side."

"And if your side wins, you're guaranteed retirement?"

She nods, and neither of us speaks about what happens if her side doesn't win. We already know the answer to that.

I sit up taller. "What can I do to help?"

"Keep Alaska safe."

I nod to Burly. "That's his job."

"But you're his father. He needs one of us with him, especially if—"

"Don't say it!"

She frowns. "Whether or not I say it, it's still reality."

"No, it isn't reality. It's a *possibility*, but it doesn't have to be a reality. This is just the struggle we have to face together to get the life we want."

"I only meant that the threat of the torture yards—"

"I said, don't say that!" My pulse drums. "I don't want to think about it. It's not going to happen."

"Okay. I'm sorry."

"Don't be. Just don't say it." I take a deep breath. "What's the plan? Are you just stopping by to run off and do more valkyrie business?"

She takes my hand and threads her fingers through mine. "I'm here to spend time with you two. I can't believe I missed four months."

"Believe it." I close my eyes. "I had to fight images of you in those yards every single day."

"It feels like I killed my target just a few hours ago."

I open my eyes. "I know. That's another reason I don't want you going back there."

Soleil kisses my cheek. "I don't want to, either."

"What now?"

"The day is ours. We can spend it here in the room or go somewhere. I still want to explore the city. Have you already?"

"No. We were going to do that together."

Her brows come together. "What have you been doing all this time?"

"Wandering the castle with Alaska, going outside to watch the unicorns. That sort of thing. Mostly, he's happy in here. The pack members have been stopping by often and usually bring toys for him when they do." I gesture to a wall lined with toys. "Also, the vampire king and queen stopped by one day with gifts and said they would help out in any way they could."

"With Alaska or the Valhalla situation?"

"Both."

She looks deep in thought for a moment. "Their forces could be useful. I'm going to have to keep that in mind. They've helped out the pack more than once."

"Yeah, but can werewolf troubles compare to Valhalla?"

"Even if not, the vampires are still powerful allies. So are the werewolves, witches, and the many creatures Tap knows."

"Not to mention dragons." I glance back over at Burly, who is staring at a wall.

Soleil nods. "It most likely will come down to the valkyries, but I'll take all the help I can get."

I arch a brow. "Even from a mesmer?"

She plants her lips on mine. "Yes, of course. Now, why don't we explore that magical, jewel-lined city?"

"Nothing would make me happier." I kiss her neck, trying to ignore the fierce emotions bubbling to the surface—the need to protect and defend her from her own kind and also the raging fury toward the valkyries and the hunters. I'll shove those feelings down for now so we can enjoy our outing as a family, but I will unleash them as soon as I'm given the opportunity.

Her enemies have gone too far, and I'm ready to make them pay.

CHAPTER FIVE

 oleil

I can hardly believe I'm walking through a dragon mall with my family—my husband and son. Alaska coos and squeals at the sights, pointing and clapping. It warms my heart. I've missed so much in the few hours I have been gone.

Months. Few hours for me, but it's been four months for them.

Four precious months stolen from me. Time I should've been here to watch my son grow and change.

All the more reason to focus on the war brewing in Valhalla. To come up with a plan to once again eradicate the hunters from the earth.

Alaska makes a happy noise, pulling me from my thoughts.

In an open courtyard, two dragons are flying around, chasing each other and breathing fire at one another. People are cheering from the sidelines, making it clear this is a show and not two dangerous beasts.

I stop the stroller, leaving plenty of space between us and the flying dragons.

Titan puts his arm around me. "Our son has an adventurous spirit. He's eating this up."

"Is that the mesmer side or the valkyrie side?"

"Probably a bit of both."

"I'm sure you're right." I lean against Titan and take in his rugged scent. I never want to leave his side again, but I know that's going to happen all too soon. All it'll take is one phone call or text, alerting me to trouble.

I shove that thought aside and focus on the dragons swooping around the courtyard, aiming fiery breaths at one another. When the blazes hit the wall, they simply disappear into the bricks, not leaving a mark.

The show ends, and Alaska starts crying. I pull the stroller away and take him over to a rainbow-colored fountain but he doesn't calm down, so I pull him out and rock him.

He reaches for Titan, still wailing.

My heart sinks, but I hand him over. Of course he wants Titan —he's the one who's been comforting him all this time. I've been absent. I'm nothing more than a picture come to life.

Titan takes Alaska and gives me an apologetic glance. Our son calms down immediately and nestles against Titan's chest. The sight both warms me and cuts deeply.

"It'll just take some time," Titan says.

I nod, not trusting my voice. Then I take the stroller and march down the hall, looking at each of the shops along the way, hoping to find something that will distract me.

Nothing does.

I hate Valhalla. Everything about the place—their rules, demands, punishments. Everything. Even the way time passes differently between the two worlds. I never asked for any of this. Never once voluntarily signed up to be an agent. It was placed on me at birth, the moment I had been ripped away from my own parents. As the child of two of the best warriors, I only ever had one path open to me.

"Stop the stroller," Titan whispers.

When I do, he lays Alaska in and buckles the straps around him.

"He was tired, that's all."

"You don't have to come up with excuses. I get it. My son doesn't know me."

Titan's expression falls. I can see the heartbreak in his eyes. "It's not like that. Alaska knows you. He's just used to me rocking him to sleep. Won't fall asleep for anyone else these days."

"It's fine."

"Soleil..."

"I said, it's fine." I blink back tears and continue on, barely noticing the shops I'd been so eager to explore before.

He puts a hand on my back. "Just give it time."

"I don't want to talk about it." A tear escapes and I wipe it, hoping Titan doesn't see it.

Doesn't work.

"Let's sit." He nods toward a bench facing another fountain.

I'm too busy fighting tears to argue with him, so I sit and look at my son sleeping so peacefully.

Titan puts his arm around my shoulders. "There isn't anything wrong with admitting it hurts. That it sucks. Valhalla stole four months from us."

I blink a few times, trying to keep my tears at bay. "From my perspective, I gave birth hours ago—less than a day ago—and he's already forgotten me. I know it's been four months for you guys. I get it."

"It just sucks."

"Right."

He kisses my cheek. "He'll warm up to you again. Look at how excited he was when you showed up. He's barely let me hold him since you arrived. Give it a few days. He'll be pushing me away so you can rock him to sleep."

I take a deep breath. "In a few days, he could be in preschool. Maybe high school."

Titan shakes his head. "We have to find a way around you going back to Valhalla. Can you put someone as your second-in-command? Someone who can go back and forth for you?"

"It's possible, but if they summon me, there isn't anything I can do about it."

"Unless..."

"What?"

"Maybe Gessilyn or the dragons can put a spell on you that will bind you to the earth. Then Valhalla can't yank you away."

"As much as I like the idea, I can't imagine it working."

Titan's expression lights up. "We won't know unless we try."

I shrug. "Maybe."

"Come on. Let's explore some more. I'll bet they have some crazy jewelry in that store over there."

"Probably." I try to smile, try to be happy for Titan. But my mind won't stop racing. Anger is bubbling inside. I'm sick of Valhalla ruling every aspect of my life. It's been thousands of years, and it's time it all stops.

Titan points out a necklace with enormous blue gems. I nod, but my mind is trying to find a way to destroy everyone on the traditional side. They need to go down.

They *will* go down.

I've had all I can take.

Everyone out to get me will regret that decision—the hunters, valkyries, and anyone else on their side.

Victory will be mine. Oh yes. It will be mine.

CHAPTER SIX

oleil

Titan and Alaska are both sleeping. I'm sure something just jarred me awake, but I don't know what. A bad dream? The sense that something is wrong?

I reach for my phone on the nightstand, moving carefully so as not to wake Titan or Alaska.

A new text from my father.

My stomach knots. That had to have been what woke me.

The phone vibrates in my hand as a second text comes in, this one from my mother.

I close my eyes and prepare myself for the worst.

Another text comes in. It has to be an emergency.

Valhalla can wait.

I reply to the latest text: *Give me a minute.*

A new one comes in.

Emergency!

Surprise, surprise.

I slide over to the edge of the bed and tiptoe over to the bath-room. My phone continues to vibrate as I make my way there. I close the door and call my mother.

"Where have you been?" she demands.

"Asleep." I don't keep the annoyance from my tone. "What's going on?"

"There are rumors of a large gathering of hunters in Alaska. Could be our opportunity to annihilate them."

"Go for it."

"Without our leader?"

I grumble. "Check it out and send word to me. I'll teleport over if it's as good as it sounds."

"Have you found other valkyries to fight on our side?"

"Not yet." I'd have to *start* looking to find any, but I don't tell her that. "Have you?"

"A few. We're spreading, but we need you. You're the leader, and there's only so much we can do with you in hiding."

"I missed four months with my son when I was in Valhalla. I'm trying to catch up."

"Don't you understand the importance of our mission? We have to take down the current leadership *and* eradicate the hunters. They aren't taking a break from trying to execute us all."

Of course she doesn't understand my need to spend time with my son. Why would she when she didn't fight for me? I bite back an irritated comment. "I'll meet you in Alaska as soon as you send word."

"You should meet us now."

"Isn't that my call, as the leader?"

The line goes dead.

I glare at my reflection in the mirror, my eyes blackening. How can my mother and I look so much alike yet be so completely different? There isn't much I can do aside from vowing to be a different mother than she is.

My phone vibrates again. I curse valkyries everywhere as I look to my screen.

It's a message from Kaja, the young valkyrie I mentored before I knew I was pregnant.

There are crazy rumors going around. What's happening?

I can't explain it over text, so I call her and fill her in.

"Do you want us to go to Alaska?" she asks. "Or El Salvador? Or wherever you are?"

I pause. "We? Who's *we?*"

"There's a group of us valkyries. We've decided to stick together since things are so up in the air right now."

"How many of you are there?"

"Just over twenty."

"Twenty?" I exclaim.

"Yeah. Things are nuts."

"How so? What do you mean?"

"You haven't seen it?"

"Not from where I'm at."

"You underground or something?"

I'm not about to admit to that. "Just tell me what's going on."

"Valkyries are falling from the sky—without lightning bolts! Just raining down, barely with enough time to open their wings and land safely."

I try to decide the best course of action. "Is your group fit to face off with hunters? I don't know yet how many there are."

"Is it true we're allowed to use our swords as necessary?"

"If you're on our side."

"We are!" Her tone holds all the resolve and excitement I should have.

"Okay, then. Head over to Alaska with your swords and meet up with the others. I'll be there soon myself."

I text my parents so they know to expect Kaja's group, then I get in the shower and prepare what I'm to tell Titan. My stomach tightens at the thought. I just returned, and now I have to leave again.

Maybe this will be the last time.

Like I'm dumb enough to believe that.

By the time I walk into the bedroom with one towel on my head and another wrapped around me, Titan's awake.

He frowns. "Let me guess. Valkyrie business. You have to leave."

"Unfortunately."

"How long will you be gone?"

"I hope not long." I trudge into the walk-in closet with clothes my size and pick out something inconspicuous and comfortable for battle.

Titan comes in and wraps his arms around me. "Any chance I can join you?"

"I'll let you know. We're checking out rumors about a large group of hunters in Alaska. So far, just valkyries are heading over to find out what's going on."

"Promise you'll stay safe?" He kisses my cheek.

"That's the plan."

He clears his throat. "If you can't get back right away, maybe we can do a video call. Alaska would love that."

I hate the thought of furthering the distance between Alaska and me, but I shove the thought from my mind. "That's really thoughtful of you. I would love that, and at least it's a possibility when I'm on Earth."

"And time will pass the same for all of us. One day will be just a day."

"Exactly. And hopefully a day is all it will be."

"You think it will?" The hope in his voice is nearly enough to break me.

"We'll see. Maybe we can beat the hunters in a day. The mess with Valhalla is going to be trickier."

"Let me know if I can join you. Plenty of people have offered to help with Alaska. He has our friends smitten."

"I'm glad for them." I turn around and look into his greenish-gold eyes. "And for you. I can't tell you how much you mean to me."

He cups my face. "You mean the world to me, Sols. I want to help with this."

Tears mist my eyes. "I'll call you as soon as I know what the situation is with the hunters. It could just be a small group, and we can wipe them out quickly. Then I'll be home before you notice I left. Or it could be a huge gathering of them and then we'll need you and others."

Titan presses his lips on mine. "Just let me know. And by the way, I'll notice you're gone the moment you leave."

I cling to him with a storm of emotions—love for him, anger and hate toward Valhalla. "I don't want to go. But if I can actually earn my retirement, we can finally live out our lives together in peace."

"We should look into finding a way to keep you away from Valhalla. You know, in case your side is less than successful. Not that I doubt you, but it's always good to have a backup plan."

I nod then rest my head against his. "I know what you mean. We need to be prepared for anything. I don't know of any way to hide from them. I'm now one of the *leaders* of the opposition. They'll want me above all others if they win."

"If there's a way, we'll find it. I'll make that *my* mission while you're out there doing the real work."

I lean back and look at him. "You're doing real work too. Keeping our son safe is the most important job we have." I glance at the time. "I'd better get going. You know, so I can return sooner."

He gives me a sad smile. "Right. It feels like you just got back."

"I did."

Cries sound from the bedroom. We both bolt over to Alaska, but I reach him first and pull him into my arms.

He snuggles against me. "Mama."

Titan kisses me. "See? He didn't forget you."

Alaska pulls on my hair. "Mama."

My legs shake. I can hardly believe it, especially after he would only sleep for Titan. How am I supposed to leave now?

I sit on the bed with Alaska, cuddling and talking to him, trying to infuse as much love as possible. Then I hand him to Titan once he gets squirmy.

I can't say goodbye. I just can't.

Once their backs are turned, I teleport out.

CHAPTER SEVEN

oleil

I text my mother again. I'm getting closer to them. Though I'd tried to teleport to her, something went awry and I wound up several miles away in the middle of some woods. For a brief moment, I thought I'd taken myself back to Valhalla's woods and lost more time with my growing boy.

Now I'm only a few minutes away from the others. I decided to walk the trek rather than use more energy teleporting again.

A clearing comes into my vision. I look around for a tree shaped like a bear—the one my mother said would be the sign that I'd found them. Relief washes through me.

I pat my sword in its sheath. "Today we'll see more action than ever before. I'm finally free to use you on anyone."

I've wanted that for thousands of years. The blade was melded with the finest of Valhalla's metals, intertwined with magic, cooled with water from a special healing lake. All that makes for one deadly sword, unlike anything available on this sphere spinning around the sun.

"Is that you, Soleil?" My mother appears from the other side of the tree.

"The one and only."

She waves me over. "The valkyries we sent to stake out the hunters just got back. You're just in time."

I follow her through the clearing and over to a little area hidden by tree branches and bushes full of ripe berries. It feels like it should still be winter in these parts, but Valhalla made me lose four months, so it's now nearly summer in the region.

My mother introduces me to the group of about thirty valkyries. I only recognize my parents and Kaja among the sea of blonde hair and varying shades of green and aquamarine eyes.

My father stands as my mother and I sit on logs. "We found their encampment less than an hour away. They outnumber us three-to-one."

"Did you hear any of their plans?" I ask.

"Only that they want to annihilate us as we did them before the other side opened and freed them."

"What's your assessment? Can we beat them as we are now, or do we need to wait until our numbers are closer to theirs?"

"I say we take them out now. Surprise them, then send them back to death's door. Now that it's permanently sealed shut, they won't be able to bother us again."

I make eye contact with everyone else. "How do you feel about that plan?"

The words barely leave my mouth before everyone jumps to their feet, fists in the air, shouting in victory.

My pulse drums with excitement. "Let's do this!"

We discuss strategy. Once we have a plan, we head over to a narrow path then follow those who already know where the hunters are staying in a single-file line.

I grip my sword. If we take out close to a hundred hunters, will that make a big enough dent in the species? We have no idea how many are out there. I've never seen so many in one place. In my experience, they tend to travel in groups of three to five.

After about a half hour, I catch up with my father. "Are we close?"

"Almost there now."

"Have you ever seen so many gathered together in one place?"

He shakes his head. "Not even when we destroyed them last time."

"Nice." And to think they've congregated in Alaska to find me.

A chill runs down my spine. Why are they so interested in me in particular? It isn't like I was leading other valkyries before this. In fact, they probably haven't even had the time to hear the news that I'm leading the opposition here on earth.

I wrack my mind for ideas. Nothing comes. I'm hardly special —hiding out for decades at a time, more interested in my non-valkyrie friends than my targets.

It doesn't make any sense. Not when there are plenty of soldiers who strictly follow orders and take out their targets in record time.

We come to the top of a hill, where an enormous log cabin comes into view in the valley. It looks like it could hold a hundred people.

My father turns to me. "That's where they're staying."

Everyone stares at me with anticipation in their eyes.

I grab my sword and hold it high. "Now!"

Several valkyries call out with war cries. Lightning bolts appear in the sky and rain down, some hitting the building and others the trees or land. Electricity races through the air. Thunder shakes the ground.

Nobody moves. They're waiting for me. Some leader I am.

I call out and race for the building, the others on my heels. We flood into the cabin.

The air inside reeks of hunters, making the hairs on the back of my neck stand on end. We wander down a dim hallway then come to a large room where the hunters are gathered together with their backs to us, all focused on one man with a golden tan and fire-engine red spiky hair.

His eyes widen and his face pales. "Attack!"

Noise echoes all around as they jump from their chairs and yell. We run for them, all aiming our swords. They definitely outnumber us by more than double. Triple was a good estimate.

I run for the nearest hunter and dig my blade through his chest. He crumples to the ground as five others surround me. I slice through another and avoid one who charges at me. Then I gut another while jumping out of the way of yet a different hunter.

Around me, the other valkyries are in the same boat—all greatly outnumbered, all battling like the fierce warriors we are.

We have this. They're falling like pesky flies.

Then a horrible piercing noise assaults my ears. Makes them ring. Sends a numbing chill through my body.

A valkyrie is down.

The hunters got one of us.

Several valkyries scream out ancient war cries. The sound reinvigorates me. Reminds me why I'm here.

I will not be taken down. The enemy will not win.

A hunter lunges for me. I kneel and hold up my sword. He falls on top of it then goes limp. I yank the sword from him and swing it at two more of his comrades. They crash to the ground.

Another piercing scream makes me freeze. Shudder.

One more valkyrie dead.

Anger rips through me. Fury takes over. Everything dims around me as my eyes turn black. My wings expand and tear my shirt. I grip my sword's handle and scream.

The hunters nearest me cover their ears and squat, squeezing shut their eyes.

I open my mouth and pull in essence. A mist appears from the mouths of the hunters gripped in fear on the ground. The essence dances toward me. Slowly.

They're fighting it.

I'm stronger. Angrier. Fiercer. A mother who wants to return home to her baby. These hunters have ripped this mama bear away from her cub.

They will not get in my way. Not today, not ever.

Finally, the essence reaches my mouth. Once it does, it flies down my throat at rapid speed. I continue drinking until they fall to the floor, limp.

I feel stronger than ever. Powerful. Ready for victory. A renewed surge of energy races through me. I hold my sword in position, ready to take down the others. All of them myself, if need be.

With one solid motion, I whip my sword around in a circle. The blade cuts through five hunters. Each one drops his weapon then crumbles.

The win is nearly ours. More of our enemy lie on the ground motionless than remain upright.

We're still outnumbered. But if we remain strong, we will be the ones to come out victorious.

The hunter essence races through me, giving me a high like no other. I leap over bodies and jam my weapon into one chest after another as I race through the room.

Now there are as many of us as them.

Another piercing yell immobilizes me for a moment. One more valkyrie down.

Something slams into my side.

I stumble but don't have the wherewithal to regain my balance. My senses return to normal, and I stop myself before tripping over one of the downed valkyries.

Something hits me from the other side.

My wings flap around, pushing against those fighting me. Hits one guy. He goes flying back.

A sharp pain slices through my arm. Everything takes on a yellow hue. The pain intensifies. It's worse than anything I've ever felt.

No. It's exactly what I felt when poisoned by the hunters before.

When I very nearly died.

Everything spins around. I can't tell which way is up. Or who the hunters are and who the valkyries are.

A man appears in front of me. He raises a sword and aims it at me. "Prepare to meet your maker!"

He lowers the blade. Green goo covers the metal.

Poison.

I'll never survive another dose of it.

It comes closer. Closer.

Nearly touches me.

I close my eyes.

CHAPTER EIGHT

itan

I pace the room, muttering under my breath. Soleil hasn't responded to any of my texts. And I've sent a lot. I mean a lot. A ridiculous amount.

She's not answering her calls, either.

Something has to be wrong. I know she left to fight some valkyrie hunters, but to go this long without responding means something has to be wrong.

It can't mean anything else.

My heart thunders out of control. I can barely breathe. I need to get myself to her.

Eveline is supposed to be here. To take me to Alaska through a rune. But she isn't here.

Where is she?

I need to figure out a way to teleport myself.

Then a thought hits me. What if Alaska can teleport? He's half-valkyrie.

No! I'm not dragging our baby into this.

I pull out my phone, this time to call Eveline. What could be holding her up? She knows how important this is.

A bright light flashes, lighting up the room. Nearly blinding me. My eyes shut, despite my best efforts to keep them open.

Once I can see, the sight before me is so horrifying I throw up in my mouth.

Soleil is lying on the floor.

Bleeding.

Unconscious.

I swallow the vomit, not allowing myself to think about how gross it is, and run to her. "Soleil!"

She doesn't respond.

"Soleil!"

Nothing.

Oh, Hades!

I shake her.

She's limp. Not responding. Maybe not breathing.

"Soleil!"

Alaska cries in his crib.

I press my finger underneath Soleil's nose.

No warm air. Nothing.

"No!"

Alaska wails.

I shake Soleil with all my might. "Wake up! You got yourself here, now wake up!"

She doesn't respond.

Alaska releases the most piercing cry I've ever heard. I have to cover my ears.

Even Burly, who never moves unless spoken to, covers his ears.

My son's screams grow louder. Covering my ears does nothing.

Maybe it'll wake Soleil.

That has to be what he's doing. I hope.

I force myself to my feet. Struggle to walk over to the crib. Pull him from it.

The noise. So loud. My eardrums are going to shatter.

Burly is on the ground, still covering his ears.

The door bursts open. Dragon shifters pile into the room, holding their ears.

I crawl over to Soleil, begging her to live with words I can't hear. The only sound is our son. He's going to leave all of us deaf if he doesn't stop.

We reach Soleil.

Alaska closes his mouth. The room goes silent.

My ears ring with a voracious tenacity like I've never before heard.

His chubby little hands reach for Soleil. He opens his mouth.

Everyone in the room cries out.

Instead of the deafening yell, Soleil's mouth opens. A purple mist swirls out of Alaska's mouth. It weaves its way to Soleil's. He leans closer, helping the mist reach her faster.

It enters her mouth.

She doesn't respond. Not even a twitch. No flutter of the eyes. Nothing.

But the essence is going in. That has to mean something. Maybe she's hanging on and has just enough strength to accept it.

I feel her wrist.

She has a slight pulse. It's weak. Barely noticeable. But it's there!

I hold my breath. Wait.

Wait some more.

Soleil's eyes open. She gasps. Looks around.

Alaska closes his mouth, cutting off the stream of essence. He claps and squeals.

I pull him onto my lap. "Soleil?"

She turns toward me. "What happened?"

"Alaska gave you his essence."

Her already-pale face loses what color it has. "Is he okay?"

I glance down at our baby, who is happily sucking on one of his toes. "Yeah, he's a lot better now than when you arrived."

She rubs her head. "I feel like I'm going to die."

I nearly drop Alaska, but manage to set him on the floor next to me before putting my hands on my wife. "What do you mean? Didn't he heal you?"

Soleil gasps for air. "He replenished my supply of essence, but I've been poisoned by the hunters again."

My heart drops to the floor and shatters. "What?"

"I need the..." Her eyes close.

"What?" I pat her cheek. "You need what?"

"The cure." Her voice is a whisper. She doesn't open her eyes.

"Where do we get that?"

"I don't..."

"Stay with me! Where is the cure?"

She just takes a noisy breath.

I turn to Burly. "Find out where the cure is to the valkyrie hunter poison! Now!"

He clamors to his feet and wildly taps his fingers on his phone's screen.

Eveline appears from a mirror. "Sorry I'm late. There was a—" Her eyes widen as she sees Soleil. "What happened?"

"Hunter poison. I don't know what the cure is."

She races over. "I know exactly where it is."

"Where?"

"A healing spring in Egypt."

I jump to my feet and lift Soleil. "I'm taking her there! You stay with Alaska."

"You can't get there without me! The fastest way there is with rune travel."

"Do you have a rune there? You couldn't use them last time we were in Egypt."

"I don't have time to explain it." She takes Soleil from me. "She needs the healing spring!"

"I'm going with you!" I pick up Alaska and give him to Burly.

He looks at me like I just handed him an explosive device.

"You know his needs more than anyone!"

"I'm a *guard*, not a babysitter."

"Then call for Iris. I'm going with Soleil!" I give my son a quick kiss before rushing over to the mirror and putting my hand on Eveline's shoulder.

"Close your eyes," she orders.

I do, and the familiar dizzying feeling sweeps over me. It stops, and before I open my eyes, I can tell we're somewhere different. The air feels different. I can't explain it any other way. It's just different. And everything smells fresh and clean, kind of reminding me of the time Soleil dragged me for a spa day.

I open my eyes and barely have the chance to take in the sights —hieroglyphics all over the walls and a shelf full of clay jars and towels—when Eveline takes Soleil down a hall. We must be headed for the spring because the sound of water bubbling grows louder with each step. I catch up with her then take Soleil from her. "Stay with us, Sols."

Soleil mumbles something I can't understand.

We come to an enormous spring. It has a fountain off to the side and a row of towels and robes lines one wall.

I turn to Eveline. "What do we do?"

"Get her in the water!"

"Right. Of course." I don't bother taking off my shoes, I just walk in fully clothed and lower myself so the water covers her up to her neck. "Now we just wait?"

She nods.

"How long does this take? Is there anything else we need to do? What happened last time?"

Eveline frowns. "I wasn't really paying attention last time. We weren't exactly friends yet, and I hadn't come willingly. Remember? Spelled to obedience. I did what I was ordered to, but that was as far as it went at the time."

"You don't remember anything?"

"I remember enough to know this is the spring that healed her from the hunter poison. She went from sick to perfectly healthy."

I glance down at Soleil and brush some hair from her eyes. "Let's hope it works just as well this time."

The water bubbles around us, but she doesn't reply. I can feel strength building within me. Hopefully that means the spring is doing its magic on Soleil.

I turn to Eveline, who is sitting across from me. "Sorry for snapping. I appreciate you bringing her here."

"It's fine. I know you're just worried about Soleil. So am I." She looks at Soleil.

"Did it take this long last time?"

"I really don't remember." She frowns, regret filling her eyes. "We weren't friends, and I never expected that we would ever be. How would you feel if your enemy forced an obedience spell on you?"

"I get it. I just wish this would hurry up."

"These things take time. Do you know how much poison she got?"

"No."

"There were a whole bunch of the hunters there?" Eveline asks.

"That's my understanding. I wasn't there. Just valkyries and hunters. She was supposed to let me know if things went south." I scoop some water and drip it onto the top of her head, hoping that'll help speed up the process.

"Maybe she didn't have time to call you."

"Maybe."

We sit in silence for a while.

Then a terrible thought strikes me. "What if this doesn't work?"

CHAPTER NINE

itan

Eveline doesn't answer my question, so I ask it again. "What if the spring doesn't work?"

"It will. Just give it time."

Time. Everything takes time. Valhalla steals time.

When will time finally be on our side? When can we spend time together as a family? As a married couple? All without having to worry about valkyries or hunters or anyone else who wants her dead?

"Are you sure there isn't something else that needs to be done? Was there something else she did last time?"

"Trust me. If I remembered anything, I would tell you."

I mutter under my breath, not wanting Soleil to hear my frustration if she can hear anything. I gaze at her beautiful face. She looks like she's only sleeping, with her hair floating around her face in the water.

"Please wake up!" I beg, not caring how desperate I sound. I'd give anything for her to be healthy. Anything.

I trace her features with my fingertip then press my mouth on hers. "I love you, Soleil. Fight! Let the healing spring take away the poison and wake up. Return to us. Please."

After a few minutes, I turn back to Eveline. "Call her mom. With so many valkyries on the planet, one of them has to know how to deal with this."

She nods and steps out of the spring without a word.

Her silence makes me think it didn't take this long the last time Soleil was poisoned.

Time drags on as I whisper declarations of my love to my unconscious wife.

Eveline hasn't returned, and I would swear it's been an hour. Hard to know for sure since I left my phone back in the dragon castle and the ancient Egyptian pyramid doesn't have clocks on the walls. I'd get up and find her if that didn't mean either leaving Soleil alone in the spring or taking her with me away from the water.

I bite my tongue, wanting to shout for Eveline. It just seems disrespectful. This whole building is probably a tomb for a long-dead pharaoh. Besides, what if yelling causes the walls to crumble?

I raise my fist and shake it, silently cursing Valhalla. If I ever find myself there, I'll destroy what I can.

Eveline returns, but she won't make eye contact with me.

"What's wrong?"

She sits at the edge of the water and plays with a nail. "There are rumors floating around about Egypt's magic possibly being compromised."

Blood drains from my body. "What? But wait. I there's magic in the water—even I can feel it."

"They're only rumors. Could be nothing more than hot air. Or maybe it only impacts valkyries."

I glance down at Soleil, still looking asleep. "Maybe. What are we going to do now?"

"I've already spoken with Gessilyn."

"And?"

"She's looking into it."

"Into what?" I struggle to keep my tone under control. None of this is Eveline's fault. "Egypt's failing magical system? Or another way to cure a valkyrie from the hunters' poison?"

"Both. Mostly the latter."

I feel slightly better knowing the highest witch on earth is working on it, but valkyries aren't from this world, so I have my doubts. "Do we know if the valkyrie hunters are from around here?"

"Egypt?"

"No. Earth. They're not from Valhalla or some other crazy place like that, are they?"

She shrugs.

I want to break something.

"I wish I knew more so I could do something, if it makes you feel any better."

"Is there *anything* you can do? You're an ancient witch. Gessilyn's the high witch, but you've been around longer. Right?"

She nods. "I've seen plenty of high witches come and go. I have the most confidence in Gessilyn out of any of them."

"But there isn't anything you can do?"

"I can try, but last time Soleil was pretty convinced only the springs could help her."

My head snaps in her direction. "What did you say?"

"That she was convinced—?"

"No. You said springs. As in, more than one."

"Yeah." Her brows draw together like she's trying to figure out what I'm getting at.

"Maybe what Soleil needs isn't in *this* one. Do you know where the others are?"

Eveline tugs on her hair. "You've got to be kidding me."

"Do I look like I'm joking?"

She shakes her head. "I'm going to have to make some more

calls. I may be old, like you pointed out, but I haven't spent any significant time in Egypt."

"Do you know anyone who has?"

"I think one of the original vampires spent some time here. Rumors, anyway. I'll call the king and queen to see what they know."

"Hurry."

She nods and heads down the hall again.

My heart shatters as I look at Soleil. She's so full of life, it's wrong that she won't wake. I study everything in and around the spring, trying to find a clue of what could be wrong. Any reason the spring wouldn't be healing her this time.

Unless the poison is so drastically different from the one used before that it'll take a completely different kind of healing. Or maybe there isn't a cure this time.

I shake my head. I'm not going to let myself even consider thoughts like that. There's a cure, and we'll find it. Soleil will help beat the hunters and the leaders of Valhalla, then she'll get her retirement and we can finally have the peaceful life we've been longing for.

Hopefully that'll happen before Alaska grows up and starts his own life.

I pull Soleil closer to me, hugging her, and run my palm over her wet hair. "We're going to get through this. You're going to heal from the poison, and we're going back home to Alaska. We're going to be a normal, happy family. Well, as normal as we can be. I'm going to fight for you. Our friends are working on this too."

The bubbling of the fountain is the only sound in the room as I listen for Eveline. I can't hear Soleil's soft breathing.

I try to think of anything else to do. Something we might have forgotten. Missed.

Nothing comes to mind.

Then a thought strikes me. It might be a little dangerous. But it could work.

My pulse drums as I consider it.

What if Soleil has to be fully immersed in the water for the healing to take place? She'd been awake last time and could've easily dunked herself under the water. Eveline might not have noticed or thought anything of it.

I pull Soleil up and whisper in her ear. "I hope you can hear me. The spring isn't working and the only thing I can think of is that your face hasn't been under. I'm going to cover your nose and mouth for a moment just so I can submerge you. I love you."

My heart pounds like a jackhammer. I hope this works and I don't make things worse for her. It's only going to be for a moment.

"I love you," I whisper.

Then I cover her mouth and nose with my hand and push her under the water until she's fully underneath. Her hair floats. Her limbs are limp.

She's still completely unresponsive.

"What in Hades are you doing?"

I turn to see Eveline, her face contorted in disgust.

"Submerging her to—"

Eveline runs toward and shoves me. I try to keep my hand over Soleil's mouth and nose so she doesn't inhale any water. Eveline grabs my hair and pulls me away from my wife. I turn and shove her away, then spin around to pull Soleil out from the water.

Something strikes me in the back of my head. Stars dance before my eyes, changing colors. I shake my head to clear it, then turn back around. "What's wrong with you? Have you gone mad?"

"I never thought you'd try to drown her!"

"And I never would!" I reach for Soleil, but Eveline pushes me under the water. I fight against her while trying to surface for air. As soon as I do, she shoves me down again. I barely get any oxygen before swallowing some water.

I choke and manage to get it out of my throat. Then I draw all my energy together and throw myself against Eveline. Once, twice, and a third time.

We both fly back, soaring over the water's surface. Then we crash into the fountain. A large crack snakes down the middle.

I pull away from Eveline and scramble toward Soleil, who is floating face-down.

CHAPTER TEN

*S*oleil

The sun rises in front of me. But it's cold. Frost reaches out for me with icy fingers. The colors of the sky crack and crumble.

My body hurts. Sharp pains run through my muscles. Dig into my bones. Nearly crushes me.

War cries sound behind me. Swords clink. Men wail in agony. A baby cries.

A baby?

I spin around, looking for Alaska. The air around me fights me. It's heavy, like water. I can barely move. Barely breathe. The air really is like water.

Where in Hades am I? Earth? Valhalla? Someplace far worse than either?

Am I dead? Have I gone to the land of dead valkyries? The place we all dread?

My insides shudder, but my body won't cooperate. The air is water.

I can't breathe.

Need air.

I flail my arms, but it does no good. The air is fighting me. Holding me down. Keeping me from breathing.

Could this be my existence for the rest of eternity?

That sounds like such a long time.

Eternity.

Swimming in the air. Struggling to breathe.

Never to see Alaska grow up. Or to kiss my beloved Titan.

Valhalla will pay if I can ever get there again. There has to be a way out. If there is, I'll find it. Nobody else has ever found it, but that won't stop me.

They have unleashed my fury.

No valkyrie will ever regret anything more than this. I will see to that.

I fight and struggle against the air. The water-like air.

Must get to Titan. To Alaska.

Away from this air.

As I wrestle the atmosphere, the watery substance fills my mouth. Trails into my throat.

Chokes me.

I cough. Sputter. Gag.

Fight.

I'm getting out of here even if I land in the torture yards.

As the water-like air makes its way down, a warm strength fills me. The debilitating pain eases.

I breathe in actual oxygen.

My eyes fly open.

Something crashes nearby. People are yelling. Sounds like Titan and Eveline.

Strength builds. Pain melts away. My lungs suck in the rich air.

I'm in actual water. Floating on my back. Hieroglyphics on the walls.

The healing spring? In Egypt? How did I get here?

I jump to my feet and look around. Definitely in the pyramid where I was healed before.

Crash!

I reach for my sword, but it isn't on me. It's back at the dragon castle.

Eveline and Titan are throwing punches. Both dripping with blood. Anger in their eyes.

I run for them. My feet don't cooperate. I fall. Hit the water's surface. Hard. Like smashing onto cement. Then I sink. Fall slowly.

Arms pull me up.

Titan. He's saying something.

Can't hear. Liquid rushing in my ears.

Eveline. Now she's speaking.

My eyes start to close again. I don't want to go back to wherever I was. Need to stay with Titan. Fight to stay here. Must not leave.

Strange colors dance before my eyes. Twisting and turning. Pulling me from my love and my best friend.

I reach for them. My hands don't actually move. I cry out. My mouth won't cooperate.

My eyelids grow heavy. Too heavy to fight.

Darkness envelops me.

I'm floating again. But I can breathe this time. Don't have to fight the air.

Someone says my name. It sounds like a song. I can see the sound bouncing along over, under, and around me.

"Soleil!" That sounds like Titan.

"Soleil!" Eveline.

I'm too tired, too warm to fight the feelings. To push against my weighted eyelids.

Must sleep. Rest. Float away.

Warmth surrounds me. The air feels like water again. Doesn't enter my mouth. But I can't breathe, either. Watery air on my skin. Nothing in my lungs.

Must fight!

I struggle. Flail my arms and legs. Kick, hit, punch. Bite. Feels like flesh.

My eyes open. Everything is blurry. Like I'm under water. Am I in the healing spring?

Are my loved ones trying to drown me? It can't be.

It can't.

I squirm and exert as much force as I can until I burst through the surface of the water. Titan and Eveline come into view again. I spit out water. "What are you doing?"

"Trying to save you!" Titan smothers me in an embrace.

"By drowning me?"

He covers my cheek in kisses. "By allowing the healing spring to do its work. You woke up, so it was a success!"

I pull away. "What in Hades happened? How did I get here?"

Titan clings to me even tighter. "You teleported to the castle after being poisoned by the hunters."

"I know. How'd I get here? Why were you two shoving me in the water?"

Eveline pulls me away from Titan and embraces me. "It was the only way for the spring to work. I was going to find another spring, but Titan thought of submersion first."

I step back. "And where's Alaska?"

"Back home."

My mind races to all the places I've called home recently. "With the werewolves?"

He shakes his head. "The castle. The servants are watching him."

"Servants?" I try to make sense of it. "Not our family? Not the pack?"

"There wasn't time. We were about to lose you."

I close my eyes and try to piece everything together. "And what about the hunters? Did the other valkyries kill them all?"

"We don't know," Eveline says. "I tried calling your mother, but she isn't answering."

"I have to get back to the castle and make some calls!"

"Let's use the rune."

We hurry to the mirror and Eveline speaks, causing the rune to glow.

Seconds later, we're in the bedroom in the castle.

The empty bedroom.

I turn to Titan. "I thought you said Alaska was here."

"He is. Maybe Iris and Burly took him outside. He loves the outdoors."

"Let's find them. I'm going to call my parents on the way." I turn to Eveline. "Can you prepare a locator spell? Just in case."

She nods. "I'm sure you'll find him, though."

Titan and I race out of the room, darting up and down hallways. My heart thunders with worry while my mind conjures up every worst-case scenario imaginable.

As if reading my mind, Titan takes my hand. "They're probably just out somewhere with him. Both Burly and Iris know I take him out a lot, that he likes to be outside the walls of the room."

"Are you sure you can trust them? You don't even know the bodyguard's actual name? Unless it really is Burly?"

He frowns. "No, that's just what I call him in my mind. He never even told me. I'm supposed to pretend he isn't there to protect us."

"I hope he's trustworthy. Where would they have gone?"

"Let's check the dining hall first." We zig and zag through some more corridors before coming to the immense eating room. Several groups are gathered at some of the tables, eating fine cuisine.

But nobody has Alaska.

My stomach churns acid.

"They might be outside," Titan says. "Or in any number of places in the castle. There's a room full of toys Alaska likes and another one overlooking a garden that has faeries tending to it."

"Maybe that's it." Then a thought strikes me. "What about that button?"

"Button?"

"The one to call for Iris back in the room."

He smacks his forehead. "Why didn't I think about that? I use it often enough. I'll run back and you can head outside."

I squeeze his hand. "I'll call Eveline and have *her* push the button. You and I will stick together."

Titan tilts his head with a funny expression.

"What?"

"I like that you're the one insisting we stick together." He gives me a crooked smile.

"I'm not leaving your side while Alaska's missing."

"He's not missing. We just don't know where he is."

"Isn't that the definition of missing?" I arch a brow.

"There's a difference. If after a good search we can't find him, then we'll consider him missing. For now, we're just looking."

"Okay." I reach into my pocket and find my phone. It's a little wet from the healing spring. I'm glad it has supernatural protection from the elements, or it'd be toast.

I follow Titan down another hallway as I text Eveline. She replies saying she sees the button and will press it. I want to ask if she has the location spell ready, but I want to stay optimistic that we'll find Alaska.

"Were you still planning on calling your parents?" Titan asks.

"I will. Let's just find our son first."

"Are you upset with me? I'm the one who handed him over to a dragon instead of a friend."

"How can I be mad when you were trying to help me?"

"I appreciate that. I'm starting to question my decision."

I stop and give him a quick kiss. "We'll find him. And I have a feeling he can take care of himself."

"What makes you say that?"

"If I remember correctly, he fed me essence. I don't think I've ever heard of a baby doing that. Sure, some young valkyries use the essence abilities without being taught, but most need the instruction."

"That is reassuring, but I'm not going to feel better until I see him with my two eyes."

"Neither will I, but it is comforting to know he knows how to use his powers. Can he use trickery yet?"

"Not that I've seen."

"You probably wouldn't, would you?"

"True. We'd better go find him. Those dragons have no idea what they're dealing with." He takes my hand and leads me down a few halls before we go through a door that takes us outside.

The pond that the unicorns like to drink from is in front of us.

Alaska isn't there, and neither are Iris or Burly.

I text Eveline, asking if she's heard from Iris after pushing the button.

Her reply is one word.

No.

CHAPTER ELEVEN

itan

I'm doing everything I can to hold myself together for Soleil's sake. I should've brought Alaska with us when Eveline took us to the pyramid. What was I thinking, handing our baby off to dragons? I don't know them, not really. Especially not that body guard. I don't even know his name! I refer to him as a nickname that I came up with on my own.

"Anywhere else we can check?" Soleil's voice pulls me from my worries.

I struggle to keep my tone even. "This castle is enormous, and I haven't explored the majority of it. They could've taken him any number of places we've never heard about."

She nods, appearing as lost in thought as I am. "Let's see if Iris has returned to the room yet, then—"

"Wouldn't Eveline have let us know if she had?" I interject. "Iris isn't there."

Her frown makes me feel bad for being so blunt, but I don't want to waste valuable time running back to the room.

"What do you suggest, then?" Soleil tugs on her hair.

"We need to find out who the next higher up is and see if they know anything. If they don't, I'm sure they have ways of finding out."

"Right. Okay. And I can call Eylin."

"Eylin?" The name is familiar, like I should know it, but I can't place it. Maybe because of how stressed I am.

"She brought us here to the city."

"Of course." It all comes back to me. "The vampire king and queen's hybrid daughter. Right. Let's just wait. Isn't she the dragon king's daughter-in-law? If she gets involved Burly and Iris could get in trouble. We don't know if they've done anything wrong."

"I kind of don't care. They have our son!"

I take a deep breath and try to think logically. "They didn't know when we were coming back. Taking him out to play isn't doing anything wrong. Let's just give it a few more minutes."

"Fine." She pulls out her phone and texts Eveline. "Still no word from Iris. Is that normal?"

"No. She always comes right away."

"Can I call Eylin now?"

"Go for it." We weave our way through a maze of hallways, checking each room we come to.

Alaska isn't in any of them.

I distract myself by looking at the artwork and listening to Soleil's half of the conversation. It's too much to bear, thinking something could be wrong. I have to believe he's okay and this is just a misunderstanding.

Soleil says goodbye to Eylin then sticks her phone in a pocket.

"What did she say?" I ask.

"She's going to make some calls for us. Said she has a direct line to the king and his highest officials in case he's unreachable."

"That's good news." But it doesn't feel that way. Every moment that passes, my regret grows. I shouldn't have handed Alaska off. I was too worried about Soleil and wasn't thinking straight—or at all.

We come to a part of the castle I've never seen and explore each room we come to.

Soleil's phone rings after a few minutes.

"Is it Eylin? Eveline? The king?"

She pulls out her phone. "My mother."

"I doubt she can help."

"Regardless, I have to find out what happened with the hunters." She taps the screen then brings it to her ear. "Where are you, Mother?"

We continue checking out rooms as Astrid speaks to Soleil. I glance at Soleil every few moments to gauge her reactions. So far, she isn't revealing much.

Then her face pales.

My breath hitches, but then I realize whatever it is probably has nothing to do with finding Alaska and everything to do with hunters.

"Thanks. I'll be in touch." Soleil puts the phone away.

"What?" I demand.

She looks at me with a wild expression.

"What?"

"The valkyries had to teleport away from the hunters before killing the rest, but that's not the worst of it."

"Of course it isn't." I take a deep breath and look down another hallway for our son. "What's the worst part?"

"Valhalla's agents are here. Falling from the sky everywhere— on each continent. Even in places where there isn't a cloud in the sky. They're here to take out the opposition."

I have several questions, but they all stick in my throat.

She nods. "I know exactly what you're thinking. Did they take Alaska?"

I can only nod. That's our worst fear because they execute all valkyrie hybrids. They call them half-breeds and look at them with more distain than they look at mesmers. And our son is half mesmer.

Finally, I find my voice. "Call Eylin back. This just went from worrisome to deadly serious."

Her eyes start to turn black. The hairs on the back of my neck stand on end. Everything in me screams to run. She may be the love of my life, but when she goes into death-mode, my body reacts like she's a mortal enemy. And for good reason. One wrong move, and she could accidentally kill me. The black has now completely covered the green and is bleeding into the whites of her eyes.

"Soleil."

She turns to me and a cold chill surrounds me.

I back away. "Calm down or I'm going to have to leave for my own safety."

Her eyes are now fully black and she seems to stare right past me. Through me. The black is now expanding out to the skin around her eyes. The air between us is heavier than a wet blanket.

All of my senses are on fire, demanding I run. Self-preservation has kicked in with full force.

"Soleil," I whisper.

Her wings appear and flap back and forth, sending a gust of wind around us.

"I'm sorry." I can't fight my instincts a moment longer.

I run.

Now our family is completely split apart, but at least I know Soleil can handle herself. She might get us kicked out of the dragon city, and she might take out everyone in sight, but she'll be safe.

Once my body calms down and I can breathe normally, I collapse on a sofa in a little reading room. A fire roars in a fireplace in front of me. My mind races.

It's hard to know what to do. I didn't want to leave Soleil, but she didn't give me any other choice. Not that I can blame her for going into death-mode. Our son is missing, and now she has to deal with enemy valkyries showing up, clearly ready for battle.

I don't know how receptive she is to communication, but I send her a text telling her to focus on the valkyries and I'll find Alaska.

She doesn't reply. Not that I expect her to in her state of mind. She might've already teleported out of here. Could be anywhere in the world.

I call Eveline.

"What's with Soleil?" she answers.

"She's in death-mode. Why, what did she do?"

"Sent me a strange text. Where are you? Have you heard anything about Alaska?"

My heart plummets. "No, and I'm assuming since you're asking, neither have you."

"Unfortunately not. Iris hasn't returned, and I've pushed the button several times. How long does it usually take her?"

"A few minutes at the most."

"I hate to say it, but something is wrong. Should I start the locator spell?"

"Please. Do you need me there?"

"No. I'll use some hair from a brush. I assume the one with the teddy bears is his."

"Yeah. Would it help if I'm there?"

"Not at all. Keep looking for him, and let me know if you find him or hear anything."

"I will. Thanks, Eveline."

"Don't worry about it. Just find the little guy."

I end the call and rise, feeling dizzy. How can this be happening? Why would Burly and Iris take Alaska? Or did someone stronger come in and overpower them? It's hard to imagine anyone big enough to defeat the bodyguard, but if anyone could, it would be valkyries.

My blood runs cold then boils at the thought. Alaska is not the property of Valhalla. They have no right to come near him. Not that they have any right to control Soleil, but that doesn't stop them from doing that, either.

I stumble over to the window and look outside at the edge of some dark woods. The trees are so menacing, it gives me chills just looking at them.

Then I see movement. People.

Burly and Iris are standing in the shadows with a bundle in a blanket.

They have him! They have Alaska.

Someone nearly as tall as Burly steps out of the woods, wearing a long black hooded robe. It covers his face, making it impossible to tell what the man looks like. His stature is what tells me he's indeed a he.

He reaches for Alaska.

Burly hands him over.

I do the only thing I can. I jump through the window and fall down toward the ground, three stories below.

CHAPTER TWELVE

oleil

"Put your wings away!" My father glares at me as if he actually has any authority over me.

I've just teleported from the dragon castle to where the opposition is now gathered in a log cabin near Anchorage, miles away from the hunters. The only thing I really care about is finding my son.

"He's right," my mother agrees. "The other valkyries will sense us from far away."

I struggle to pull in my wings and lighten my eyes. "How many Valhalla agents are we dealing with?"

They both shake their heads. Nobody knows.

I glance around the tiny room with the remaining valkyries after the altercation with the hunters. We lost nearly a third of our numbers. We took out more of them but also left a lot more.

"What are we going to do about the valkyries?" Kaja frowns. "Between them and the hunters, everyone wants us dead."

"I need to get back and find—" I stop myself before saying *my son*. Even though these valkyries are all on my side, I can't trust them with the knowledge. Not yet. Maybe not ever. The less who know about him the better. If someone weak gets tortured, they could end up telling Valhalla's leaders about Alaska. Or they could say something to the hunters. "There's something important I need to find."

"More important than this?" asks a valkyrie whose name I can't remember.

"Yes!"

My mother shakes her head. "No, it's not."

I glare at her, anger pulsating through me. But how can I expect her to understand? She never raised me. Never knew what it was like to watch over and protect her child. "Yes, it is."

We stare each other down.

My father steps between us. "We need to focus on our mission, and you're leading us, Soleil. *This* is your priority."

I bite back a scathing comment. "You two seem to have everything under control. Why don't you deal with the agents?"

He shakes his head and steps closer. "Because you're in charge."

"Doesn't appear that way to me." I take a step toward him.

His eyes narrow. "You took the responsibility."

"It was hardly my first choice." I clench my fists.

My mother steps between us. "Reports are coming in from all over the world about agents pouring in. There have been a couple earthquakes and even a volcano rumbling and steaming. This is bigger than any of us."

Her words rip me in two because she's right. If the agents aren't stopped, there won't be an Earth for Titan, Alaska, and me to call home and live as a family. My hands shake, so I stuff them into my pockets before anyone notices. "Do we have any others in the opposition? Is it just us?"

Both my parents step back. My father answers me. "There are groups growing in every inhabited continent."

"And they each have a leader?"

He nods.

That means any one of them could step up to be the top leader of the opposition. It doesn't have to be me.

"That doesn't change the fact the judges approved you as the head here on Earth."

I hold back a groan. "Of course it doesn't. What do we need to do?"

"Aren't you supposed to tell us that?" asks one of the valkyries.

"Leaders aren't allowed to ask for advice?"

She gives me a blank stare.

I take a deep breath. "Welcome to a democracy. That's what you want, right? That's why we're fighting the other side, isn't it? To earn our freedom and stop living under the thumb of a dictatorship."

Nobody says anything. I also don't know where we should put our focus. The idea of killing other valkyries makes me sick, but it has to be done. If we don't, they kill us or drag us back to Valhalla for endless punishment.

I stand tall. "We need to join forces with more of the opposition. The question is, do we go to them or have them come to us? Either way, we all need to gather together somewhere."

My mother nods. "We'll start making calls."

Everyone else pulls out phones and reaches out to the other valkyries. Apparently I'm the only one who doesn't know any outside of this group.

Someone recently told me that I'm not as renegade as I like to think. Clearly, they're wrong, or I'd be making calls along with everyone else here.

With everyone distracted, I whip out my phone and send a text to Titan.

Have you heard anything about Alaska?

I wait for a response, but none comes. The message doesn't even show that he's read it yet. Hopefully, that's good news. I hate myself for leaving before we found Alaska, but given I'm still bound to Valhalla, I'm not left with another choice.

While the other valkyries are busy figuring out what's going on in the rest of the world, I decide to call Toby. Nobody in the opposition will be happy about the idea of accepting assistance from any of Earth's supernatural creatures, but I don't care. Chances are, we'll need all the help we can get, and I have access to the best of the best—the vampire royalty and their armies, the world's werewolf leaders, the high witch and her family, and now even the dragons. And that doesn't take into account all the unreachable that Tap actually knows.

"Soleil, is everything okay?" Toby answers.

I walk away from the other valkyries and in a quiet voice fill in Toby on everything, including my missing son.

He lets out a low whistle. "All your worst fears coming together at one time."

"Exactly." I clench my jaw.

"I'm sorry to hear it. We'll drop everything to help you. What can I do?"

I clear my throat, hating to ask for help. "Would you be able to call the other alphas? This is happening everywhere. Valhalla's agents are here for death."

"Anything you need. One question, though."

"What is it?"

"Are we able to kill valkyries? Death is your business, and your people aren't even from here."

"Valkyries can be killed, but it's a matter of acting quick and getting them by surprise. And if their eyes turn black, just run. Make sure everyone knows that. Black eyes mean get out as fast as possible. I'm not going to lie to you, Toby. This could be more dangerous than anything you've ever faced." My stomach clenches at the thought of anyone in the pack getting hurt on account of this. "Actually, I probably shouldn't have called. You should weigh this out before deciding to help."

"It's no question. We'll join your fight, Soleil. You're family. We just need to know what we're walking into. All we know about your kind is what you've told us, and that really isn't much."

"It's never been an issue until now." I tell him as much as I can think of and promise to let him know anything I think of later.

"I'll be in touch after I speak with the other alphas. Are you going to call Gessilyn and the vampires?"

"And Tap and anyone else I can think of. Do you think Eylin would be able to reach the dragon leaders?"

"If anyone could, it would be her and her husband."

"Do you think they'll help?"

"The dragons?" Toby asks. "The world is about to be under attack—that sounds like the exact thing they would help with. They'd be in their element."

"Perfect. Thanks for everything."

"Glad to help. Things have been pretty boring lately, anyway." I can hear the teasing in his voice.

I almost smile. "Thanks, Toby."

We say our goodbyes, then I join the others to see what progress they've made before I start calling anyone else.

Kaja comes over to me. "There are some large concentrations of the opposition in Europe and Asia, however not much action here in the Americas. At least, none anyone has been able to find yet."

"Keep trying. I have some more calls to make." I don't mention my calls have nothing to do with other valkyries.

She nods and pulls out her phone.

An hour later, I've spoken with everyone I can think to call. Everyone wants to help and is pulling together resources I don't have access to and promises to brainstorm ideas with their leaders.

A commotion from the other valkyries sounds just as I'm saying goodbye to Eylin.

I rush over. "What's the matter?"

"They've already begun." My father rubs a mark from his blade.

"Where?"

"Egypt." He slides it into the sheath. "And there are reports of earthquakes in South Africa. They have to be doing something there, as well."

"Don't forget the volcanic activity in Italy and New Zealand." My mother paces. "It's hard to know where to focus."

"Easy." I squeeze my sword's handle. "We're going to Egypt. That's where they're attacking. But I'm going to need someone to give me a little essence so I can teleport *and* fight."

My father places a hand on my shoulder. "There isn't time. I'll teleport you with me."

Before I have a chance to text anyone about the latest developments, my father and I travel and end up in the middle of a desert. Heat beats down, and sand is the only thing visible in any direction.

CHAPTER THIRTEEN

itan

I curl into a ball and roll as soon as I hit the ground, ignoring the cuts all over my body. None are too deep. Then I jump to my feet and immediately make myself look like an enormous fire-breathing dragon. I race toward the man in the hood about to take my son.

His eyes widen—finally visible as I near—and his jaundiced face pales at the sight of me. Or, more accurately, my trick. He grabs the bundle then runs into the forest.

Anger and fear both tear through me. I wish I could actually transform into a dragon. Instead, I'm limited to how fast my own two feet will take me. And I can't see all that well in the dark woods. With his dark hood, it makes it even more challenging to follow him.

But I manage. He has my baby, so I have no other choice. Letting him get away isn't an option.

Getting Alaska back is my only option.

I trip over a root sticking up, but manage to keep my balance. But it puts more distance between me and the hooded creep.

He zigs and zags around as though he's been through these woods many times and knows it by heart. Has he been planning this all along? And more importantly, what does he want with my son?

I push myself and close the distance between us, but it isn't enough. They're still too far ahead. Out of my reach.

"Stop!"

He doesn't. Not that I expected him to.

I trip over another root, and this time, I slam into a tree. The bark scratches my face and my ears ring upon impact. By the time I stand and shake off the surprise, the hooded man along with Alaska are out of sight. I still can't hear anything other than the ringing.

No matter. I know the direction he was headed. I race to catch up with them.

Can't see them anywhere. I come to a fork in the path. Light shines in the distance from the trail to the right. An even deeper darkness swallows up the one on the left.

I hesitate. The hooded man would probably go toward the darkness. Or would he expect me to think that, and actually go toward the light?

Either way could be right or wrong, and standing in place is the one thing that guarantees I won't reach them. I have to choose something.

But which one?

A soft cry sounds.

I know that cry. Without a doubt, it's Alaska.

They've gone toward the light.

My feet spring into action seemingly on their own.

Alaska cries again.

Fury surges through me, giving me extra energy and strength. I push branches out of the way and leap over exposed roots, finally able to see them as I make my way toward the light.

I step out of the woods and into a muddy field.

Neither my son nor his kidnapper is there. But there is a set of fresh footprints.

I follow them, nearly losing my shoes in the process as the thick, sticky mud clings to them. I round a corner then come to a grassy field filled with colorful wildflowers.

A hooded figure runs out of my sight.

My muscles burn as I race after the man.

Alaska's cries now pierce the air. He sounds pained.

My stomach tightens and my feet move faster. The distance between us closes again. I'm almost to them. The man's heading for the woods again.

Not on my watch. I push my legs as fast as they will go.

The hood is closer, closer, closer. Now just out of reach.

I gasp for air and reach for him. My fingers barely miss.

Alaska's wails push me to keep going. To force my body to the edge of its limits. My muscles and lungs burn, but I refuse to slow down. To even consider it.

I reach for him again. Make contact.

He leaps ahead. Out of reach again.

I take a deep breath and lunge for him. Crash into his back. Dig my shoulders into him. He stumbles. Slows. Clings to Alaska.

My breath hitches. I steady myself. Grab onto his cloak. Squeeze. Cling to it.

He yanks back. His arms flail. My son falls.

Everything else fades from my sight as I focus on him. Reach for him. I'm too far.

The bundle moves in slow motion toward the rocky ground.

I can't get to him in time. Can't move fast enough.

The man is falling. Going to crash on top of Alaska, crushing him over the rocks.

"No!" I can't stop it. Can't reach them.

Alaska squirms. The blanket flies off. He lands on his feet.

Wait, what?

I crash to the ground. The wind flies out from my lungs. As I try to drink in oxygen, I stare in disbelief at my son.

He lets out a howl that sends a shiver down my spine. Glares at the now-downed hooded figure, his eyes darkening. He shouts gibberish. Eyes grow darker. His voice gets louder and the made-up words faster.

The hooded man pushes himself up to sitting.

I try to lunge for him but still can't breathe. Can't get any air.

Alaska kicks him in the chest. Then again. His shouting intensifies. His eyes are deathly black, the color bleeding to the skin around his eyes.

Death-mode.

The hairs on the back of my neck stand on end. Somehow, I manage to suck in some air. Then some more.

The hooded man reaches for Alaska. I lunge for him, but my son extends a palm toward me.

I can't move.

Alaska opens his mouth. The hooded creep freezes. His mouth opens. A purple mist swirls out. Dances toward my son. Flies into his mouth with such a force it should send him back twenty feet.

He doesn't budge.

I can't move, either. His palm is still holding me in place from four feet away.

The essence continues with the force of a firehose. As Alaska drinks it in, he grows. His clothes tear apart until they fall to the ground in shreds and he looks four years old instead of the four months he actually is.

The hooded kidnapper falls to the ground.

Alaska drops his hand to his side.

I crash onto the dirt at the sudden release of his hold. Dirt embeds in the wounds I sustained from jumping through the window.

Grunting, I push myself up and dust off what dirt I can.

Alaska turns to me, his eyes quickly fading back to green.

I stare at him, unable to speak. Not only does he look different —older—but I'm stunned by what I just saw.

He rubs his hands on his legs. "That takes care of him."

My mouth falls open. "You can speak?"

"Yeah. Where's Mommy?"

"She had to teleport away—she didn't want to leave you again."

He frowns but doesn't say anything.

I take off my shirt and step toward him. "You'd better wear this until we can get you some clothes that fit."

He arches a brow, but lets me put the oversized shirt on him. "What about this guy?"

"I'm pretty sure he isn't going to give us any more problems."

"Should we bring him back to the castle?"

"No. I'll let Burly know about him. He'll know what to do." I pull out my phone and snap some pictures of the guy and the area to show Burly.

"Okay." Alaska shrugs, making the shirt fall off one shoulder.

"Let's get back to the castle." I fix the shirt as best I can.

"Do you know the way?"

"Mostly." I shake my head, still trying to get used to the fact that my four-month-old looks like he should be getting ready for preschool. "Do you want me to carry you?"

"Not now."

"Okay, then." I glance over at the hooded dude to make sure he hasn't come back to life, then head back for the woods. I'm surprised at how easily I remember the way back, especially given how distracted I was.

When we break through the trees and the castle comes into view, I notice Burly and Iris are standing exactly where they were before. And they don't act like they see us.

"Hey, Iris!" Alaska jumps and waves his hands in front of her face.

She doesn't respond, doesn't even blink.

Alaska turns to me and tilts his head. "What's going on?"

I wave my hands in front of Burly, also not getting a response. "It's like they're under a trance."

"Iris!" Alaska shoves her.

"Hey!" I snap. "Don't ever hit a girl."

"I *didn't*. I'm trying to wake her up!"

"As long as you don't hit her." I take out my phone and call Eveline.

"Where are you?" she answers.

I tell her. "Hurry, and bring all the magical stuff you have."

CHAPTER FOURTEEN

itan

Eveline runs over, gasping for air, her dark hair flying behind her. She stares at Alaska. "Is that Alaska? It can't be."

"It is. Long story."

"You found him! That's great news. But why'd you tell me to bring my supplies?"

I glance at Burly and Iris. "They're in some kind of trance."

She steps closer and studies them. "They sure are, and you're right to think it's magic-induced. I have little experience with dragon magic, but let's see what I can do."

"I need to get Alaska and me cleaned up. Any chance we can get them up to the room in this state?"

"They'll probably only obey whoever set the spell."

"Even if he's dead?"

Eveline's brows draw together. "You killed the dragon who did this?"

"He did." I nod toward Alaska.

Color fades from Eveline's face. "Seriously?"

Alaska nods, a proud smile slowly crossing his face.

"I'm impressed. Whoever did this was capable of some really strong magic."

"Wait." I hold up a hand. "Alaska inhaled all of that dude's essence. Any chance he possesses some of that power? Even just for the time the guy's essence is in him?"

"Maybe." She kneels and studies Alaska. "Do you remember me?"

He nods.

"Do you think you can give me a little of that scary man's essence?" Eveline holds out her palms.

"Probably." Alaska closes his eyes, scrunches his face, then opens his mouth. Purple mist swirls out, collecting just above Eveline's palms.

I hold my breath, half-hoping he will grow younger as he releases the essence that aged him. Soleil will be so disappointed that he got even older while she was gone.

When he closes his mouth and opens his eyes, I finally breathe.

He looks exactly the same.

"Thank you, Alaska. You did great." Eveline gives him a quick smile before rising and facing Iris and Burly.

I take Alaska's hand. "We should get cleaned up, little man."

"Can't we watch this?"

"Don't you want to find your mom?" I ask.

"After."

"Okay." I pull out my phone and text her that Alaska's safe. She's probably too busy fighting hunters or valkyries, or both, to come back, anyway.

"Thanks, Daddy!" He wraps his arms around my legs.

I pick him up and hug him, stepping back from Eveline and the magic.

She has the swirling essence close to her face and she's whispering to it.

"What's she saying?" Alaska leans forward.

"Her spells are usually in a different language. We wouldn't be able to understand, anyway. I don't want to get too close."

"Why not?"

"It could be dangerous."

"So can I."

His comment sends a chill down my spine, but I don't want him to know. I kiss his cheek. "You're a sweet little boy, Alaska."

He doesn't take his attention away from Eveline. "You saw what I did to that bad man."

"Doesn't change the fact that you're still a sweet little boy."

Alaska doesn't respond.

"You are." My voice comes out gruffer than I meant, not that he seems to notice.

Eveline holds the essence out toward Iris and Burly, then blows it on each of them.

Iris is the first to blink. She looks around in a dazed confusion. "What happened?"

Alaska squirms out of my hold and races over to her. "We saved you!"

She gives him a double-take. "Alaska?"

He nods, his proud smile returning.

Iris throws her arms around him. "Thank you."

Burly still looks in the trance. Maybe the magic takes longer since he's enormous.

Just as I start to think he's going to be a permanent fixture at the entrance to the woods, he finally shakes his head. "How did we get out here?"

I pull out my phone and find the pictures I took of the hooded kidnapper and show him. "This guy put you two under a spell. Does he look familiar?"

Burly's face pales.

The fact that the kidnapper scares him makes my stomach knot.

Burly turns to me. "He did this? Who killed him?"

I gesture toward Alaska. "My son."

"What?" Burly exclaims. "That's not possible."

"I saw it with my own eyes. And that's how he aged."

He looks back and forth between Alaska and the picture. "Impossible."

"It's not. I swear."

Burly looks at me. "That man has been on the most-wanted list for years. Nobody's been able to catch him, much less kill him."

"What can I say? My kid is one of a kind. Kidnapping him was that guy's last mistake."

"He's still there? Where you pictured him?"

I nod. "On the other side of these woods."

Burly's forehead wrinkles. "I need to inform the king and retrieve the body. I'll send for another bodyguard to watch over you while I take care of this."

I glance over at Alaska. "I'm pretty sure we'll be okay on our own."

"The king will have my head if I don't."

"By all means, send someone."

He pulls out a phone and slides his finger around the screen as he runs into the woods.

Iris turns to me. "Are we going back to the room now?"

"Yeah. I've got to get Alaska and myself cleaned up. Will you be able to find some new clothes for him? None of his other stuff is going to fit."

"Of course. No problem." She gives a little bow.

As we head for the castle, I check my phone. Still no response from Soleil. She hasn't even seen my text.

I hope she's alive.

And I hate myself for thinking that, but with a war like no other ever seen before, what else am I supposed to think? The traditional valkyries and the hunters all want her dead.

"You okay, Daddy?"

I turn to Alaska and try to smile. "Yeah, of course."

"Thinking about Mommy?"

"Yeah, but she's strong. The best of the best."

He nods. "Best of the best."

Once inside the castle, I do my best to ignore the sideway stares everyone in their fancy clothes gives me. I'm not only shirt-less, but cut and covered in dirt. Not to mention the fact that Alaska is wearing my torn, dusty shirt that is way too big for his body.

When we reach the room, Iris opens the door for us. "If you don't need anything else, I'll find some clothes in his size."

"That would be wonderful. Thanks."

She bows, studies Alaska, then leaves.

I pull my shirt off my son, still unable to believe how old he looks, and try not to let him see my astonishment. "Let's get you in the bath."

He looks me over. "What about you?"

"I'll get a shower when you're done." I take his hand and lead him into the bathroom, where I start the water in the tub so big it could fit a family.

He splashes in the bubbles and has as much fun as I'd expect from a kid his size. Yet he's actually less than half a year—and to Soleil, less than a week old. My chest tightens at the thought of her seeing him now. She's going to be crushed. But this time, we've both missed out on those years.

I'm not sure if that'll be a consolation or not. My guess is not.

After a while, Alaska yawns. "I'm getting sleepy."

"Do you want a nap?" I don't know if my kid still naps.

"Yeah." He yawns again.

"I suppose growing that fast would tire you out."

Alaska nods then rubs his eyes, getting suds in them. He cries like I'd expect a child his age to, but it seems so far removed from killing his kidnapper by essence drinking.

I grab a fresh washcloth and get the soap from his eyes, then I towel him off. When we get out to the bedroom, no one is there. But I can tell Iris has been and gone because there are a few child-sized outfits lying on the bed. I take the set of pajamas and help

Alaska into them. "Do you want a snack or anything before you lie down?"

He shakes his head and rubs his eyes again, this time not getting anything in them.

I help him into the bed and tuck the covers around him. He's already snoring.

My body nearly gives out. I lean against the wall, not wanting to get any dirt on the covers, and take several deep breaths. My mind reels, quickly replaying everything.

What a trip.

Knock, knock!

Burly comes in, giving me a small nod. "Everything is taken care of."

I'm not fully sure what that means, but I nod in return. "Thanks."

"You can get cleaned up. I'll watch him."

I hesitate. "What happened before? How did that creep get Alaska?"

Burly frowns. "He used a powerful magic. The king's magicians have covered me with a spell to protect me against it. They're doing the same thing to Iris right now."

I glance at Alaska, not wanting to step into the bathroom.

"There won't be a repeat of last time, sir. You have my word."

Knock, knock!

"Come in," I call.

Eveline walks in.

I wrack my mind, trying to remember where she went after waking Iris and Burly from their stupor. I can't remember. "What's going on?"

She closes the door behind her. "I spoke with one of the dragon witches, and she explained the magic used against them. I'm prepared to fight against it if anyone shows up trying to use it." She studies me. "You'd better get those wounds cleaned up before they get infected."

"He doesn't want to leave the child," Burly says.

Eveline sits on the edge of the bed with a fire in her eyes. "I'll guard him with my life."

I believe her. "Thank you."

"Go on." She waves me away. "Before I have to use magic on those cuts."

I head back into the bathroom and check my phone.

Still nothing from Soleil.

CHAPTER FIFTEEN

oleil

Blood splatters onto my face. I blink just before it gets into my eyes. Then I yank my sword out of the traditional valkyrie I just eliminated. Gasping for air, I wipe my lids then look around.

Two valkyries crash to the ground before me. Sand flies through the air as two more wrestle just out of my reach. Lightning streaks across the sky and more of Valhalla's finest drop from the sky.

Like we weren't already outnumbered before. Even with multiple groups of the opposition joining forces in Egypt, we're no match for the other side. Not going by sheer numbers.

We need to pull out and rethink this. Find more to join our side, at the very least. That was our plan before the others came to Earth, eager to fight us before we were ready.

Something strikes me in the back of my head. I lunge forward as a sharp ringing noise echoes in my head. My sword nearly flies from my grasp, but I cling to the handle. After regaining my footing, I spin around, swinging the blade.

The valkyrie, who I assume is the one who struck me, ducks. But not quickly enough. My blade slices off her ponytail. She reaches up to feel it, her eyes blackening. Before she has time to do anything else, I dig my sword into her chest.

"Soleil!" Ellika points behind me.

I whip around, swinging my sword before I have time to figure out what's going on. The blade slices off the head of a valkyrie in position to dig her weapon into my neck.

She crumbles to the ground.

The sky turns black. Thunder shakes the ground. Everything lights up as dozens of lightning bolts zig-zag across the horizon.

Blood drains from my body.

Valkyries rain down from the sky.

I lift my sword. "Retreat!"

One by one, valkyries from the opposition disappear. As the leader, I wait.

Rain pelts down, soaking my clothes, running down my raised weapon.

Valhalla's valkyries double in number as more descend.

Most of the opposition's forces have left. I'm ready to teleport out when I see one of mine with a sword to her neck.

Kaja.

I feel doubly responsible for her, having been her mentor before all this began.

Several valkyries run at me. War cries sound from every direction.

My throat goes dry.

Kaja screams.

A deadly blade is coming my way. Aimed directly at my heart.

I close my eyes. Teleport to the spot Kaja stands a hundred feet away. I place my hand on her shoulder and teleport us away just as a blade cuts into my shoulder. Blood trails down my arm, soaking into my shirt.

When I open my eyes, I'm in the dragon castle. In the room I share with Titan. I was trying to teleport back to Alaska, the state. But I must've been thinking Alaska, my son. When wasn't I?

Eveline, who is sitting at the table, stares at me with wide eyes and a pale face. "Soleil?"

I gasp for air and cover my new wound. No words will come.

She leaps from her chair. "What happened?"

I'm too weak. Between the fighting and teleporting, I can't speak.

Eveline holds her palms over Kaja and me, speaking in an ancient language. I think I used to speak it. Too hard to remember. My eyes close.

A soft warmth massages me. Weaves its way through my body. Whispers to me. Says it loves me.

What?

I force my eyes open and turn my head.

Titan is kissing me. "Please be okay."

"Titan."

He meets my gaze. "What happened? Where were you?"

"We were outnumbered."

His expression contorts. "Hunters or valkyries?"

"Valkyries."

"When are you going to let me help you?"

I moan, unable to find more words. Pain still shoots through my shoulder, yet Eveline's magic is still working its way through me.

"Do you want me to wake Alaska?"

I halfway sit up. "You found him?"

Titan nods and rakes his fingers through his hair. "It's kind of a long story."

"He's safe?"

"Most definitely."

I close my eyes, allowing the relief and Eveline's magic to continue healing me. The stabbing in my shoulder weakens and most of the rest of my body feels strengthened. I give it another minute before opening my eyes. "Where is he?"

"Napping." Something in Titan's expression gives me pause.

"What's wrong?"

"Nothing. He's healthy and strong."

I struggle to sit. "What aren't you telling me?"

He frowns.

"I knew you were hiding something." I try to stand.

Titan puts his hands on my shoulders. "I need to tell you what happened first."

Worry seizes me. I picture him maimed and permanently disfigured. "What?"

He takes a deep breath. "Do you promise to fully hear me out before you react?"

"This doesn't sound good."

"Please. Do you trust me?"

I nod and glance over at Kaja. She's sitting up, speaking with Eveline.

Titan threads his fingers through mine. "A dragon shifter with strong magical abilities overpowered Burly and Iris—"

"My name is Stan," Burly interrupts.

Titan gives him a double-take. "Can I keep calling you Burly? It's more fitting."

"As you wish."

"Stan," Titan mutters and shakes his head before turning his attention back to me. "Anyway, the magic put him and Iris in some kind of trance. The dude took off with Alaska—"

I gasp.

"But not before I saw him. I jumped through a third-story window and chased him through the woods behind the castle."

My heart thunders and I struggle to breathe. I remind myself that Alaska is safe and napping.

Titan rubs a gash near his ear I hadn't noticed. "That's how I got cut up. Anyway, that's not the important part."

I trace the wound and kiss it. "It is important."

"Not once you hear the rest of the story." He takes a deep breath and tells me about his difficulties chasing them through the woods and nearly losing them. Then he gets to the part about our son defeating his own kidnapper who managed to overpower the bodyguard.

I lean against Titan. "I knew Alaska was special, but that's even more than I imagined."

"There's more." The tension in his voice makes me stiffen.

"What?"

Titan takes a deep breath and takes what feels like a century before speaking. "He aged right before my eyes as he drank in the essence. I don't know if it was the fact that he took in so much or because it was magical."

"How old is he?"

"He's still only four months old."

"How old does he look?" I ask.

Titan licks his lips and won't make eye contact. "About four."

He may as well have punched me in the gut. "Four years?"

"Yeah. It was instantaneous."

I struggle to find words. "Does he act like a four-year-old or a baby?"

"Like a preschooler. He's capable of a full conversation."

Everything spins, making me dizzy.

Titan wraps his arms around me. "I'm sorry. I wish I could've stopped it. You've already missed out on the first few months, now this."

I twist my hair into a knot. "There's nothing you could've done. At least he's safe. That's the only thing that matters."

"He was asking about you."

"He remembers me?"

Titan kisses my hand. "Of course."

"That's good news, at least."

"Do you want to see him?"

"More than anything."

Titan helps me up and we walk over to the bed, where a little boy is sleeping in the middle. Not just any little boy. Our son. The baby I just had. Now a preschooler.

How can this be?

Titan kisses my cheek. "I'll be right back."

I just nod, then I sit on the bed and scoot closer to Alaska, careful not to wake him. It's definitely him—just older. Bigger. He has all the same features.

It's hard to take in. I haven't been gone long. Less than a day.

What's going to happen the next time I have to leave? It'll probably be soon. I should've teleported back to the base with the rest of the opposition.

I don't want to miss any more time. Not another moment.

Titan sits next to me and rubs my shoulders. "He's beautiful, isn't he?"

I nod and quickly wipe my eyes. "Looks just like you."

"And all I see is you." He brushes his lips across mine. "I just spoke with Eveline. She's going to watch Alaska."

"I'm not going anywhere."

Titan traces my jawline with his fingertips. "We're going to get you some food, but not here. Alaska needs it quiet to sleep. His body has a lot to recover from."

I shake my head. "I'm not leaving." My stomach rumbles.

He lifts a brow.

"I don't care if I'm hungry."

"I do. And he'll be fine."

Eveline comes over. "I won't take my eyes off him. I promise."

My whole body aches. I just want to snuggle next to my son and sleep as long as he does.

"We'll come back soon." Titan helps me off the bed.

Kaja turns to me. "I'll join the others and let them know you're healing. That you'll be back soon."

"I appreciate it."

She closes her eyes and disappears.

Titan pulls me out of the room and as soon as the door closes behind us, he wraps himself around me and kisses me deeply. "You have no idea how worried I was. I kept trying to reach you."

"The battle was intense. Like nothing I've ever seen."

A pained expression covers his face. "I take it the war is far from over."

"Unfortunately."

"And the hunters?"

"Still out there, bent on killing every single one of us."

He kisses me. "Maybe you guys should lay low for a while and let the hunters duke it out with the other side. Let both your enemies lower each other's numbers while you grow your forces."

"I'm not sure that'll work."

"Why not?" He kisses me again. "I think it's the perfect plan. It'll also give us some time together before you have to fight again."

"Maybe."

He puts his arm around my waist and pulls me into the nearest room. It looks like the one we've been staying in, but is empty. He stares at me with hungry eyes.

My heart skips a beat and suddenly, nothing else matters. We just got married and have hardly had five minutes alone together in that time. Our son is safe, being watched by a strong dragon shifter and Eveline, a powerful witch who nearly overpowered me a lifetime ago. At least it feels that long ago.

I trace the wound on Titan's face and notice it faintly trails down his neck and under the collar of his shirt. "How badly did you get hurt?"

"Hardly at all. And the dragon's salve is healing everything quickly."

I unbutton his shirt and push it off his shoulders, tracing the cut down to his side. Now I see the damage for what it really is. He has gashes all over his stomach and chest. I trace those too. "This is from jumping out a window?"

"Third story." He flexes, then winces as a scab cracks.

I kiss it. "And you didn't hurt yourself otherwise? No broken bones from the landing?"

He shakes his head. "I barely remember touching down. My focus was on Alaska."

"And you saved him." I trace another cut, then kiss him and allow myself to forget that anything else exists other than the two of us.

CHAPTER SIXTEEN

 oleil

I wake feeling better than I have in a long time. Strong and healthy. Able to defeat a throng of enemies.

Maybe.

But for now, I just want to enjoy a little down time with my family. Unfortunately, a *little* time is all I'm likely to have. My phone is back in our bedroom, and I'm sure it's been going off like crazy. Hopefully it hasn't woken Alaska—if he's still sleeping. I have no idea how much sleep he's going to need to recover from growing so much in a matter of moments.

I scoot closer to Titan and kiss his cheek. "Morning," I whisper, though I'm pretty sure it's evening. Hard to say for sure with the way time has been passing lately.

His eyes flutter. He smiles, the skin around his eyes crinkling. "This is how I like to wake up."

"Same here." I kiss him again. "Are you ready to see if Alaska is awake?"

Titan stretches. "Yeah. But wait, I never fed you like I promised."

I hold back a laugh. "I think we got a little distracted."

He smiles devilishly. "That we did. You'll have to distract me again real soon."

"Oh, I plan to."

Titan leaps on me, kissing me deeply. We roll around, managing to knock things off the headboard and the two nightstands in the process.

I get up and pick the comforter from the floor. "Maybe we should pick up in here before we check on Alaska."

"That's why they have servants, silly." He kisses my cheek, then we get ready in the bathroom before heading back to our room.

Burly is standing next to the door and Eveline is reading a book to Alaska by the window. He jumps up and wraps his arms around both of us.

I pull him into my arms and swing him around. "I've missed you so much!" I want to ask if he remembers me, but part of me fears the answer despite Titan telling me Alaska hasn't forgotten.

"Are you here to stay, Mommy?" Alaska pleads with his eyes.

It pulls on my heartstrings like nothing else. More than anything I want to tell him I'll never leave, but I can't do that to him. I struggle to find the right answer.

Titan pats his head. "She's here now, and we're going to have breakfast together."

"Yippee!" Alaska squirms to the ground and runs around.

I laugh, hardly able to believe the sight.

Iris leaves, saying she'll be right back with some breakfast foods.

Alaska runs in circles, pretending he's flying.

I turn to Titan. "Just watching him makes me tired."

"You and me both."

We laugh as he picks up speed. He's running so fast, he looks like a blur of colors in the shape of a boy.

I bump Titan with my hip. "I think he gets that from you."

He snickers. "You sure about that?"

"Yeah." Not that I can remember being that young, nor is there anyone I could ask about my early childhood.

Alaska continues running around at top speed until Iris returns with the food. She sets it on the table, then he jumps onto a chair and smiles, not even slightly out of breath.

"Have fun?" I smile at him as I sit.

He nods as he reaches for a boiled phoenix egg.

"Do you need help with the shell?" Titan asks. "Those are tricky."

"Nope-a-roo." Alaska taps the egg on the side of a plate and pulls off the top half then the bottom half.

Titan and I exchange surprised glances. He turns to Iris. "Have you ever seen anyone do that?"

"Can't say that I have. Do you need anything else?"

He shakes his head. "I think we're fine, thanks."

She gives a little bow then picks up around the room.

Titan grabs a pastry. "I hate to ask, but do you have to run off and take care of valkyrie business?"

"Unfortunately. But I'll stay with you two as long as I can, though I doubt it'll be long enough."

He kisses my cheek. "We'll take what we can get. And I'll do what I can. Join forces with the pack or whatever. Battle at *your* side."

I give him a sad smile. "I wish that were possible, but it's too dangerous with the valkyries. I don't want to risk losing you. However, you've more than proven yourself to be smarter than the hunters."

"So, you'll let little ol' me help with them?" Titan teases.

I frown. "It's the valkyries that worry me. You know it's not personal. We're more powerful than most creatures here on earth, and you mean more to me than anyone else. You and Alaska. I just want you two safe."

"I'm definitely safe with him around." Titan ruffles Alaska's hair.

"Hey!" Alaska giggles and reaches for another boiled egg.

My phone buzzes. I ignore it for a moment, but then I look because I have to. I'm the leader of the opposition, after all.

The text is from my mother. It's short and to the point.

Hunters are migrating toward Seattle.

My blood runs cold. They're heading for the pack, who live just a ferry ride away from there. They know exactly how and where to draw me out.

"What is it?" Titan's expression is taut. "You have to go?"

"The hunters are headed for Toby's mansion."

Titan's mouth drops. "Do they know?"

"Not yet." I find my texting conversation with Toby and give him the news. "Now they do."

"What are you going to do?"

I sit up straight. "The hunters want me. I'm going there, and I'm going to face off with them."

"By yourself?" Titan jumps from his chair. "That's insane! You realize that, don't you?"

"Not alone. The opposition will be there, as will the pack. But if they're headed there anyway, I see no reason not to act as bait."

"Have you lost your mind?"

I narrow my eyes. "No, I haven't. And I don't appreciate you saying that."

His mouth forms a straight line. "You know I think the world of you, but bait for the hunters?"

"Why not? Draw them all to one place, then get rid of them once and for all. The other side is permanently sealed. They won't be getting out again. Between the opposition and all the supernaturals I know—including you—we can beat them. Then it'll be easier to focus on Valhalla's agents."

Texts flood my phone. Toby and my mother both want to know my plan. I tell them we'll meet at the mansion, exactly where the hunters expect me to be. My mother says she'll pass on the word to the rest of the opposition and Toby agrees to spread word to Tap, Gessilyn, and beyond.

"When are you heading over?" Titan asks.

"It's going to have to be soon. The only question is what to do with Alaska."

He glances up at the mention of his name.

"There is no question." Titan shakes his head. "He's coming with us."

I give him a double-take. "To battle the hunters?"

"To be close to us. He can stay with the other kids in the pack."

"Other kids?" Alaska whips his attention to us, nearly dropping what's left of his egg.

"The whole point of being here is to keep him safe. If Valhalla gets wind of his existence..." I let my voice trail off as I shudder at the thought. They wouldn't think to give it a second thought. They'd simply eliminate him.

Titan nods. "Perhaps Laura will take all the pack kids—and he's one of them since you're a pack member—to Tap's safe area. That isn't far from the mansion."

"I suppose that's true. I still hate the idea of taking him from here."

"He's not a hundred percent safe here, either. Remember what happened when we went to the healing spring?"

I nod. How could I forget my baby being kidnapped? It was only a day ago, even though now he looks four years old.

My mother texts me again.

They appear to outnumber us.

I draw in a deep breath and hold it.

"Not good news, I take it?" Titan lifts a brow.

I shake my head. "We need to go now."

"I'll gather my weapons." He gets his things ready as I text back and forth with my mother and with Toby.

Before long, we're ready to leave. Almost.

"I'm going to need essence to teleport us."

"Use mine." Titan opens his mouth.

"Sorry." I shake my head. "It's like a fine wine, a delicacy. It'll mess with my mind not unlike alcohol. I can't."

"What, then?"

Burly steps forward. "You can take some of mine."

"No, me!" Alaska tugs on my hands. "I took lots from that bad man."

I exchange a glance with Titan. I don't know how I feel about taking essence from our son.

"Lots of magic." Alaska nods quickly.

"Is that why you have so much energy?"

Alaska shrugs.

"Is it safe?" Worry lines crease Titan's forehead.

"I've never had any problems drinking essence from another valkyrie."

"From a four-month-old?"

"Hey." Alaska puts his hands on his hips. "I'm no baby."

"Technically, you are." Titan gives him a knowing look before turning back to me. "And he's not a full valkyrie."

My phone buzzes with more texts.

I glance back and forth between Burly and my child while my phone continues alerting me of more impending danger. The dragon shifter was overpowered by the magic of the kidnapper whereas my little hybrid killed the same man.

I kneel down and look Alaska in the eyes. "I'm going to take a little of your essence. Just enough to get us over to the pack. Is that okay?"

He nods his head quickly. "I have lots!"

From the corner of my eye, I see Titan tapping his foot and his arms crossed. I ignore the sting of guilt for doing something he doesn't agree with fully. He'll see it'll be fine. I'm barely going to take any from Alaska, and with his overabundance of energy, he clearly needs the release of it. This is for the best all around, especially if Titan insists on bringing our son with us to the mansion.

I take a deep breath and stand to face Titan. "I can't do this knowing you aren't happy. I wouldn't do anything to hurt him. Ever."

Titan gives a little nod. "I know. I trust you. Just because I don't like this doesn't mean I don't believe in you. We're making the best of a bad situation. Let's just do this."

I give him a quick hug, then kneel in front of Alaska again.

He opens his mouth, clearly ready for the exchange of essence. At least someone is.

I open my mouth and pull, waiting for his essence. It surprises me as being a mixture of purple and green. I can't help but wonder if the green is because of him being a hybrid or if it's from the magic.

Either way, I'm struck by its strength the moment it weaves down my throat. I cut off the flow almost immediately. He's already given more than I need.

"Did you get enough?" Titan asks.

"Plenty. Let's go." I put my hands on them, close my eyes, and picture the mansion.

CHAPTER SEVENTEEN

itan

I open my eyes to find myself in the middle of the living room in the mansion. There are about a dozen pack members all staring at us wide-eyed.

"Sorry." Soleil dusts herself off. "Did Toby fill you in on what's going on?"

Everyone talks at once.

Alaska clings to me, the overwhelm obvious in his eyes. I pick him up and reassure him everything is fine. "These are friends. Family. Should we find the kids?"

He nods, wrapping his arms around my neck in a chokehold.

I loosen his grip and head for the kitchen, where I find Laura cooking what smells like meatballs and spaghetti sauce.

She smiles when she looks over. "Great to see you again, Titan. Who's this little one?"

Alaska buries his face against my shoulder.

"This is Alaska."

Her eyes widen. "My, my. He grew up fast, didn't he?"

He peeks at her. "You know me?"

"I know your parents."

"Oh." He nestles against me again.

Laura steps closer. "There are some kids about your age. Do you want to meet them?"

"Maybe." Alaska's voice is muffled against my chest.

"They're really nice. And they have a whole toy room."

Alaska turns fully toward her. "Really?"

Laura nods and gives him a friendly smile. "If your papa doesn't mind watching these meatballs for me, I can take you upstairs and show you the room. I'll bet that's where the kids are."

Alaska looks at me. "Can I?"

"Of course."

He reaches for her, then she carries him out of the room, turning to give me a reassuring smile.

I stir the food and listen to as much of Soleil's conversation with the pack from the other room as I can. Most of the werewolves sound eager for the confrontation with the hunters. I'm not afraid to face them, but I'm not excited about the prospect. I just want them out of our lives. To stop trying to kill my wife. That's why I'm here.

Hopefully, this will take care of them for good then the opposition can focus on winning the civil war without the hunters making things harder for everyone.

The conversation in the living room quiets. I strain to hear what they're saying. I'm tempted to walk away from the food, but I don't dare risk ruining a werewolves' meal.

After what feels like forever, Laura returns. "He's playing happily with the other kids."

"Is anyone up there with them?"

She nods and takes the spatula from me. "Both Victoria and Katya. They're expecting, and will be sitting out this battle. Toby said they might stay with Tap, depending on how things go."

My breath hitches. "And they're okay with taking Alaska?"

"He's part of the pack." Laura opens the oven and checks on something in there.

"Thanks for everything."

"My pleasure." She smiles at me before turning back to the meatballs.

I follow the hallway to the living room, but before I reach it, Astrid steps in front of me.

"When did you get here?" I give her a double-take.

She ignores my question. "We need to talk. Now."

The look on her face makes my stomach flip-flop. "What's the matter?"

"Not here." She nods toward the front door. "Grab your sunglasses."

I didn't bring any, so I march outside and squint in the bright sun. "What's going on?"

"Werewolves have exceptional hearing. Let's go near the woods."

"Why don't you want them to hear?" I struggle to keep the irritation out of my tone.

"Oh, you'll find out."

"Great."

We cross the immense property and reach the edge of the woods.

I turn to her and narrow my eyes. "What's so important?"

She returns the glare. "Your wife is expecting again."

It takes a moment for me to process the news. "What? Are you sure?"

"I can sense these things. Are you two trying to outperform rabbits or something?"

"Don't judge us."

"This is the worst possible time!" Her nostrils flare. "You do realize she's leading the opposition here on earth?"

"Of course I do! Don't act like I secretly planned this. You really think I want to put her through all that again?"

We stare each other down until she speaks. "I've never heard of a valkyrie conceiving so easily. I don't know what's going on."

"Perhaps it's a dual-breed thing. What does it matter? Does she want to step down now?"

Astrid's brows furrow. "She doesn't know, and she's not going to."

My mouth drops open. "You've got to be kidding me! Of course she needs to know. Do you remember how fast things progressed last time?"

"With any luck, we'll defeat both sets of enemies before she figures out what's going on."

My mind spins. "Again, do you remember how fast everything happened before?"

"Most everything happens in the last week. That gives us a solid three weeks."

I slap my forehead. "Are you for real? She needs to know so she can take care of herself and the baby."

Astrid shakes her head. "She can continue on, business as usual. It won't be a problem."

"This isn't for you to decide! I'm going to tell her." I turn toward the mansion.

She speaks in what sounds like Norwegian. A breeze whips around me. Only me. No leaves move.

I spin back around. "What did you just do?"

"Nothing." Her expression tells me otherwise.

"Whatever." I hurry toward the house, expecting Astrid to race past me and insist I keep the news to myself.

She doesn't.

That should probably worry me, but I'm too upset to care. Soleil is pregnant again? So soon? When I married a valkyrie, I really had no clue what I was getting myself into. I figured I was in a little over my head, just the fact that our species are different.

By the time I swing open the front door, the living room is packed full of werewolves, valkyries, vampires, and a mixture of other species.

I weave through the crowd and find Soleil speaking with Toby, Gessilyn, Tap, the vampire queen, and another valkyrie. I hesitate, not wanting to interrupt but also needing to tell her the news. She deserves to know, despite what Astrid said. She needs the whole picture as she steps into war.

Soleil excuses herself from the conversation and comes over to me. "Are you okay? You look like you've seen a ghost. That might actually be good. We could use all the help we can get." She smiles.

I don't. "There's something you need to know."

"What?"

I open my mouth. Nothing comes. I try to tell her about the baby, but not a sound escapes.

Astrid. She did this to me. I don't know how, but she did.

"What is it?" Soleil asks.

I try again, but my voice won't work. I even attempt to tell her without using the words pregnancy or expecting.

Nothing.

Soleil tilts her head. "Are you feeling sick?"

Astrid joins us and puts her hand on my shoulder. "I think he's feeling a little tongue-tied, aren't you?"

I glare at her.

"We were just talking, weren't we?" Astrid's tone is smooth as honey.

"Yes," I grumble.

"Oh, good. You found your voice." She smiles.

I try to tell Soleil about the pregnancy, but can't.

"Poor thing." Astrid pats my back. "Anyway, I was just telling Titan I've heard news from Valhalla. Things are really intensifying up there. There have been catastrophic losses on both sides, but there is good news."

"What?" Soleil asks.

"More valkyries are joining the opposition every day—both there and here. Word is traveling fast, and our people want freedom. We have more hope now than ever before."

"Really? That's the best news I've heard all day."

Astrid beams. "Don't be surprised to see more valkyries joining us today."

I turn and glare at Astrid. My fists clench, my jaw tightens. I don't think I've ever wanted to punch someone so badly before, and that's saying something.

Toby enters the hallway. "I just got word that the hunters are near. They've just disembarked the ferry. They'll be here within the hour."

Soleil nods. "I'll go out first. Alone."

I try to object.

My voice won't cooperate.

CHAPTER EIGHTEEN

 oleil

I grasp my sword's grip with one palm and the doorknob with the other. My heart thunders and my hands shake, but I smile trying to convince myself more than anyone else that I can do this. Step out to meet what is likely the world's concentration of valkyrie hunters.

Alone.

They knew I'd be here. Probably knew I'd bring other valkyries with me.

One thing they don't know is that I have a child. That's something they're never going to find out.

"We're right behind you." Toby adjusts one of the guns across his chest. "They won't get close enough to hurt you."

I nod. "Of course not."

Titan looks like he's going to explode. I can barely glance his way. Each time I do, he pleads with his eyes. He doesn't want me to do this.

I don't want to do this. If there was another option, I'd take it in a heartbeat.

My mother gives me an encouraging smile and nods. "You'd better get out there, daughter."

I want to run past everyone up the stairs and give Alaska another kiss.

As if reading my thoughts, Gessilyn speaks. "The protection spell I placed on the children will make it so the hunters can't see any of them as long as they stay in the room. We're right behind you."

Toby glances at his phone. "They're almost at our property line."

The look on Titan's face nearly drives me to tears. Before I give in, I spin around and storm through the door. March across the porch and down the steps.

Before my shoes touch the grass, I see the hunters. Actually, it's the cloud of dust they've kicked up. They've nearly reached the gate. It won't keep them out.

I hold my head high and make my way over, keeping my mind on the small army of supernaturals in the mansion. More of them hiding in the woods that surround the property.

Once I draw the hunters into the open yard, werewolves, vampires, witches, and other strong supernatural creatures will surround the hunters. They won't be able to run. Only fight.

The dust clears on the other side of the gate. Faces appear. I recognize several. I've seen them all over the world.

I wave them over. "Come and get me!"

Though my heart thunders, I hold my sword high. There's so much more at stake now than there ever was before. A husband and a son. I keep both of their faces in my mind as the hunters break down the electric fence and race toward me.

Three hunters reach me first. I slice my blade through the neck of one and stab the next one in the chest. They both fall to the ground. The third evades my strike and swings a sword at me. Our blades meet with a loud clink. We get into a sword fight, dancing around as more hunters swarm the property.

As they do, vampires and other creatures surround us from the woods. Werewolves swarm the yard from the mansion. It's hard to tell who outnumbers who, but war cries fill the air along with grunts, groans, clanging of swords, and gunfire.

Hunters surround me, leaving me no room for escape. There are five or six of them. I swing my weapon around. Take one out. Duck and barely miss being struck by a baseball bat. Jam one in the knee with my sword. Something hard hits my arm. Then my back.

I jump up and swing my sword around in a circle and manage to knock two of them to the ground. That still leaves me outnumbered. I continue fighting until I find myself on my back with four of them piled on top of me, striking me with their fists.

Anger surges through me. My wings fight to burst out as I'm crushed on the ground. Pressure builds on my eyes as they blacken. I open my mouth and pull in essence as quickly as I can. The essence fills me quickly and visions of their lives flash through my mind as though I'm experiencing them for myself. They're a bloody, violent bunch. Not that I'm surprised, given the throbbing bruises all over my body.

Finally, one after another they fall on top of me. The disturbing images are still racing through my mind as the essence flow wanes. I shove them off and jump to my feet, trying to shake the movies of their lives. My wings flap and stretch now that they have room to expand.

As far as I can see, the entire property is filled with fighting. Swords and bats swinging. Vampires biting into necks. Werewolves and other shifters in their animal form attacking the hunters. A jaguar howl echoes through the air, sending a chill down my spine. The sky lights up a sparkly orange for a moment—must be a witch's spell. The air has the metallic smell of blood and death.

Three hunters run for me. My insides churn with the overabundance of essence. I can't take in more without making myself sick. I still could grow ill with the poor quality of essence pulsating through my body.

That leaves me with only one option. I open my mouth and expunge the essence raging through me at those bent on killing me. My bruises throb all the more as the newly inhaled essence flies out. It knocks over one hunter as it weaves into his mouth. He struggles until he goes limp. Essence enters the other two and they crumble.

I barely have time to catch my breath when I see more hunters pour onto the property from the road. Now we're definitely outnumbered, maybe two-to-one. And more are coming still.

They had to have sent word to every hunter on the planet to come here. That's the only explanation.

Something hard strikes me in the side of my head. Stars dance before me and a sharp ringing bounces through my head. My grip loosens on my sword's handle. Warm liquid trails down my face. Everything spins around me.

The hunters will not win. They will not overcome me.

I grasp onto my handle before it drops. Wipe the blood from my face. Glare at those trying to kill me while clinging to the images of Titan and Alaska. We *will* live a happy life as a family. A quiet, undisturbed life.

Nobody will get in the way of that. Not the hunters, not Valhalla.

I scream out a primal war cry as I swing my sword and drink in more essence. More disturbing images fill my mind. As much as I try to ignore them, they're overpowering. Like I'm living several lives all at once.

The essence stops. The images slow. My attackers have fallen to the ground.

I gasp for air. My stomach lurches from all the negative, dirty essence. It's too much for a valkyrie like me. Those who enjoy killing can deal with it so much more easily.

A fist strikes my cheek. Another my back. A shoulder. My chin. The right temple. Nose. Stars shine before me. Everything spins.

My sword falls. Shouts sound. A fist to my eye. Everything takes on a red hue. Yellow. The ground is coming closer. More assaults on my back as I fall. Everything is moving in slow motion.

The hunters around me freeze in place. Some in mid-strike. Others as they lunge for me.

I must be hallucinating. My arms hit the ground first, protecting my body. My knees hit next. Then my elbows. It's like my body is trying to protect my stomach.

My stomach.

No.

It can't be. Not now. Not again. So soon.

Before rising, I press my palm on my stomach. It's curved just slightly. Barely noticeable, but it is.

A new surge of energy pulsates through me. One more reason to fight. My mind swims with the new knowledge. Another baby.

We *just* got married.

Then I notice the hunters are still frozen in place.

Eveline is standing just beyond them, holding her arms toward them. She looks at me. "Hurry!"

That explains the colors and them freezing, mid-strike.

It takes me a second to shake off the surprise of that and the news. I can't think about the pregnancy now. I swing the sword and take out each of the hunters held by Eveline's spell.

She drops her hands and wipes her forehead. Then her face pales.

I turn in the direction she's looking. Even more hunters are piling in through the now-destroyed gate.

Eveline and I exchange a worried glance. We're far outnumbered now. I don't dare to venture a guess as to how much. It's a lot. More than I'd thought possible.

Now would be a great time for more supernaturals to pile out of the woods.

They don't.

Ziamara taps my shoulder. "Drink my essence. You need it."

I rub a bruise on my cheek. "I can't."

"You said vampire essence is especially strong. Hurry!"

I can't deny that I need healing. Her essence would help a lot. "Okay."

"Good." She opens her mouth.

I drink it in, and the soft sweet essence massages me as it makes its way down my throat. The pain from my wounds ease until they're fully gone. Until I feel good as new.

She blinks her eyes a few times. "Not sure I'll ever get used to that."

I start to say something, but then she lunges for me.

No, not for me. Behind me. She takes down a hunter inches from me.

More are marching my way.

With Ziamara's essence strengthening me, I feel like I can take them all. I pick up my sword and shout in victory.

I swing my weapon, taking out enemy after enemy until my sword grows heavy. Until my arm can barely hold it up.

That's when I notice the colorful sky. It isn't from a witch's spell. The sun is going down. We've been out here fighting for hours. Given that everyone looks as exhausted as I feel, I'm not surprised.

We all need rest. Food. Water. But the hunters still outnumber us. How much longer can we keep this up?

I swing my sword at a hunter lunging for me. He drops to the ground. Another comes my way and I aim for him. My hand slips. The weapon wobbles. Falls toward the ground. My hands ache.

No time for fatigue. Must keep going.

I lunge for my sword and grasp it before it hits the ground. Cling to it. Shove aside my exhaustion. I can rest later. After the hunters have been eradicated.

Two enemies fall as I swing my weapon. Several others rush at me, all swinging spiked baseball bats. I aim my blade at one of them and the others swarm around me.

Shots ring through the air. One hunter goes down. Then another and another.

Titan steps forward. "Are you okay?"

I wipe some blood from my cheek. I think it's from a hunter. "Never better."

"Good. I've been trying to get to you since this all began."

One of the downed hunters lifts a gun. Aims it at Titan.

He pulls the trigger.

CHAPTER NINETEEN

itan

I barely have time to register that a gun is aimed at me when it explodes with a loud bang.

Soleil throws herself against me. My pregnant wife is trying to save me. She doesn't even know she's carrying our second child. My heart thunders and I push against her, trying to get her out of the bullet's path.

Something hits me. Not something. Someone.

Astrid.

She shoves us both out of the way. Red sprays from her shoulder. She crashes to the ground. Grabs her wound.

The hunter aims his gun at Soleil.

Rage like I've never felt runs through my veins. I jump over Astrid and smash into the hunter, knocking the gun out of his hand. It flies through the air and hits another valkyrie.

She spins around and grabs it from the air, then looks around.

"Him!" I shove the hunter toward her.

The valkyrie shoots him in the chest. He falls to the ground.

More hunters swarm Soleil as she tries to help her fallen mother.

I take what energy I have left and make myself look like a lion. I roar, and though I just sound like myself, the others hear an actual lion roar.

Each hunter attacking Soleil freezes and turns in my direction, terror covering their expressions. One wets himself.

I lunge for them. They scatter. I race after them, shooting until my gun needs to be reloaded again. I'm nearly out of bullets at this point. And to think I'd stockpiled enough to last years. All used up in this one skirmish.

As I turn back to help Soleil, something catches my eye. I freeze in place. It takes me a moment to register that I'm not imagining what I see. As I stare, my trick fades and everyone sees me as I really am.

Alaska stands on the porch.

My son is outside. Watching the bloody chaos. This will scar him for life, if it doesn't kill him.

I burst into a run, leaping over fallen supernaturals and hunters. I gasp for air, my heart about to explode from worry.

Must protect him. Get him inside. Back to whoever was supposed to be watching him.

What if the hunters got inside? Attacked the children?

Before I reach him, Alaska stands up tall and spreads out his hands. His eyes turn black and he opens his mouth.

An unseen force knocks me to the ground. I try to rise, but can't get up. My feet are twisted together and something or someone presses on my back.

I look up to Alaska, willing him to be okay.

He's alone on the top step. Massive waves of essence are weaving and dancing toward him. There have to be hundreds.

All the nearest hunters are frozen in place, essence leaving their bodies. Heading straight for my child.

I flash back to him with the kidnapper. It's like that all over again, only monumentally worse. Instead of one person's essence, he's going to inhale hundreds.

And I can't do a single thing about it. Nothing to stop it. He may even be the one holding me down.

What is he? How can he be so powerful? Because he's a valkyrie hybrid? Or something to do with the combination of mesmer and valkyrie?

The swirls of essence whirl toward him, building a wind as they move. Then they crash into his mouth, making him stumble back a few steps.

I reach for him, but my arms won't move.

Soleil cries out from somewhere behind me.

Gasps sound from all around. Supernaturals attack the unmoving hunters. They fall to the ground, and as they do, their essence dissipates. Doesn't reach my child.

The enormous wave of essence pouring into his mouth shrinks little by little. It gives me almost no relief. Not when so much is still making its way into him. I know firsthand what too much essence does. I've seen the effects on Soleil—a fully grown valkyrie.

What will it do to a small boy?

I regret the question as soon as I think it.

Alaska's clothes rip and tear. Fabric flies away from him. He's growing again. In front of so many witnesses.

We won't be able to keep him or his nature secret any longer.

Everyone is about to find out what he is. All these valkyries will know.

Valhalla kills valkyrie hybrids.

I struggle to break free of the invisible force holding me down. It presses harder the more I fight it. I fight all the harder, but whatever is holding me down is stronger than anything I've encountered before.

The essence continues flowing in Alaska, who now looks twice as old as he did when he stepped onto the porch. Nobody would ever believe he's only four months old. Not when he looks eight years old. Scratch that. Now he looks ten or eleven.

Maybe that'll be what saves him. Who would believe Soleil was pregnant with that boy just months ago? I hardly believe it myself, and I've seen every change he's gone through.

The force holding me down eases. Doesn't let go entirely, but I am able to halfway sit up. Barely.

All at once the essence snaps away from Alaska, the hunters collapse, and I'm free from whatever held me down.

I leap to my feet while my son stumbles backward, wipes his mouth, and looks around at the field of living and dead supernaturals. He wipes some hair from his eyes.

Alaska now stands nearly as tall as me. He's got chiseled muscles and facial hair. The only clothes on him are what's left of his now too-small pants.

This can't be happening. My stomach churns acid.

Someone turns to me. "Wasn't he a little kid a minute ago?"

"That's crazy talk," I say quickly.

"Yeah." He nods.

Now I just have to convince everyone else of the same thing.

Silence hangs in the air. My ears ring after being in the midst of such an intense battle.

Someone puts their hands on my shoulders. Soleil. The shock in her eyes matches the feelings raging through me.

She tugs on me. "We've got to get him inside!"

"Right." I'm still in shock. My back aches from the force that weighed me down. "I tried to stop him, but I think he held me down—while taking in the essence."

"I felt it too."

"You did?" I give her a double-take. If Alaska can hold her back, what exactly is he?

We race to the porch, darting around and over people, then usher him inside. Soleil doesn't stop once we're in the entry. She takes him upstairs to our bedroom and locks the door behind us.

"What just happened?" She stares at him as though trying to convince herself the young man in front of us is actually our child.

The one who only feels a few days old to her since Valhalla made her lose most of his first four months.

"We won. They didn't kill you. I saved you, Mommy."

Her mouth falls open. Tears shine in her eyes.

"You're not happy?" He shivers.

I take off my shirt and hand it to Alaska. "Here, you can wear this."

He doesn't take it. "Did I do something wrong?" The pained look in his eyes is more of the little kid he just was than the almost-man he is now.

"No, of course not. The hunters are dead and your mom is safe. We're all here together."

Soleil wipes away a tear. "How'd you get outside? You were supposed to be in with the other kids. Victoria and Katya were supposed to be watching you."

He shivers again.

"Put on the shirt." My voice comes out gruffer than I meant.

Alaska does as he's told then sits on the bed and sighs. "I was with them, playing with the toys. But I was curious about the fighting. They were playing music, but I could hear everything outside, anyway. When I went to the bathroom, I looked out the window and saw it all."

Soleil buries her face into her palms. "I didn't want that."

I put my arm around her.

Alaska continues. "But when I saw it, I knew I could help. I just knew. So I went out and focused my attention on the bad guys' essence. I drank it in."

Soleil looks up at him, tears clinging to her lashes. "I didn't want you seeing their memories. They're horrible."

"See their memories?" He wrinkles his forehead. "You mean those funny movies, Mommy?"

She buries her face again. "Can you call me Mom? You look too old to be calling me Mommy."

Alaska turns to me, his innocent eyes wide. "Did I do something wrong?"

My heart shatters. I clear my throat. "No, nothing. This is a huge adjustment for all of us. That's all."

He frowns then turns to Soleil, who still has her hands to her face. "I'm sorry, Mommy. I mean, Mom."

"She's not upset with you," I tell him. "It's everything else."

"I'm growing up too fast."

I can't deny that. "It's not your fault."

"I drank the essence."

"All for good reasons."

He tugs on his hair. "Why does it make me grow? Is that normal?"

Soleil wipes her eyes and looks at him. "To my knowledge, there's never been anyone like you. We don't know what's normal."

"What am I?" He looks back and forth between us.

Soleil and I exchange a glance then sit on either side of him. She tells him about her life as a valkyrie growing up in Valhalla, then I tell him about life as a mesmer.

"So, I'm both?" Alaska asks.

"Yes." Soleil's voice cracks. "A hybrid."

"Why does that make you sad?"

She looks away.

He turns to me. "Why?"

I consider my words. Do I tell him straight or cushion the blow? He looks old enough for the full truth, but he's so young.

"Dad?"

"Valhalla doesn't tolerate valkyrie hybrids."

"Oh..." He holds his breath, clearly processing the news.

I wrack my mind for something comforting to say.

Alaska sits up taller. "I'm stronger than them! They can't hurt me."

Soleil rubs her eyes. "Valhalla's leaders aren't like the hunters. We need to stay away from them."

"I'm not afraid of them."

We sit in silence. Soleil presses a palm on her stomach, reminding me of the secret I can't talk about. Will our second child have a normal childhood? Or are we dooming any of our offspring to the life Alaska has been forced to deal with?

He breaks the silence. "I can fix your owies, Mom."

"What?" She rubs a bruise near her eye.

Alaska turns to me. "You too, Dad. I can heal you both."

Before I can object, he opens his mouth and essence flows out. It splits in half and enters both my mouth and Soleil's. As the silkiness runs down my throat, a tingle spreads throughout my body, intensifying at each wound until I feel as good as new. Better, actually. I've never felt stronger.

Knock, knock!

I picture Odin on the other side, ready to snatch my family away from me.

"Hold on." Soleil wipes her eyes again then unlocks the door.

The door opens and Astrid steps inside, her expression solemn.

My stomach squeezes. "Does everyone know about Alaska?"

She shakes her head. "The valkyries just think he's from Valhalla. Some are whispering that he's a direct descendant of Odin."

Soleil frowns. "I guess that's good. At least they don't think he's a hybrid."

Astrid stares at her. "That's the least of our concerns."

"What do you mean?"

She leans against the door. "A valkyrie just arrived from Valhalla with news that half the castle has been decimated. It's really bad up there. Everyone has escaped the torture yards. Utter chaos would be a massive understatement."

"Are we winning?" Soleil asks.

"I'm not sure anyone is." Astrid takes a deep breath. "And the judges are asking for you."

Her nostrils flare. "They want me to return to Valhalla so soon? When things are out of control? So dangerous?"

I jump to my feet. "There's no way! I won't allow it!"

Astrid glares at me. Obviously, I'm too close to sharing the secret. I don't care. Soleil should know exactly what the stakes are.

"You'd risk me and your grandchild?" Soleil rubs her stomach.

My mouth falls open. She *does* know.

Astrid's brows come together. "Did he tell you?"

Anger surges through me. "How could I? You've prevented me from saying anything!"

Soleil looks back and forth at us, stopping at her mom. "Is that true?"

"It was for your own good."

"I'm thousands of years old, Mother! I can handle the truth! Not that I need you hiding it from me. I figured it out on my own."

"You have the gift of sensing the unborn too?"

"Or I'm aware of my own body! I'm not going to Valhalla."

Astrid shakes her head. "You can't make that decision. You're the leader of the opposition down here."

"Not if I abdicate and put you in charge."

"Doesn't work that way. The judges approved of your position."

Soleil crosses her arms. "If there is no real leadership among the valkyries, I don't see how that counts for anything. I'm not going."

"You have to."

Alaska steps between them. "I'll go for her."

"No!" Soleil, Astrid, and I all say at the same time.

He narrows his eyes. "I can do it."

I shake my head. "Not happening."

Alaska steps closer. "I want to protect Mom. I've already shown I can do it."

"Here! Against hunters, not against valkyries—in Valhalla!" I can't believe I'm having this conversation. He should still be in diapers, barely sitting up, yet here he is staring at me almost at eye level.

Astrid opens the door. "It's time."

"I'm going." Alaska grabs the door. "Mom's carrying my sister. I'm not letting her go there."

We all exchange wide-eyed glances. How does he know Soleil is carrying a girl? Just a guess, or something more?

Soleil gasps. "They're taking me now!"

Alaska wraps his arms around her. "Not without me!"

I reach to pull him away.

CHAPTER TWENTY

Holding my breath, I open my eyes. I'm the only one on the bridge to Valhalla. Just me. Titan managed to keep Alaska back.

I wait just a moment to make sure he hasn't followed me.

Bang!

The bridge shakes. I hear stone crumbling on the other side. More than half of the castle is gone. Nothing more than a pile of rubble. War cries sound in the distance. Various parts of the sky light up different colors.

Bang!

Everything turns black for a moment. Another castle wall falls.

I press my palms on my stomach and hope for the best. I'm not showing and hopefully won't until all of this is over. With any luck, anyone with the capability to sense pregnancy will be too distracted to notice.

Was Alaska right about this baby being a girl? Is that even possible? My mother looked shocked when he said that. If she's never heard of anybody predicting that, then Alaska is more of a unique creature than we thought before.

My back aches with a dull pain running up and down my spine. I ignore it and hurry across the bridge, stopping only when another bang makes it unstable.

I need to get in and out as quickly as possible. I can't risk missing out on any more of Alaska's childhood. If months pass before my return, how old will he be then? Twenty? Fifty? A hundred?

Once I reach what's left of the castle, I expect the giant, red-eyed guards to question me.

They aren't there.

In the thousands of years I've come back and forth, I've never once seen that.

A shiver runs down my achy spine. Yet I still feel extra-strong since Alaska gave me essence back in the mansion.

Bang!

The castle walls shake as the sky lights up green.

I leap away, not wanting to get caught underneath falling stone. Nothing crumbles. Not yet. It's only a matter of time, given the shape of the other side of the massive structure.

A bloody, one-armed valkyrie limps past me, looking behind her. Screams and shouts sound from that direction. Then I see the soldiers. They chase the maimed valkyrie to the bridge. As they near her, she jumps.

Her screams grow quieter until they disappear altogether. If the rumors are to be believed, she'll fall and never stop.

I shudder and run around the building, hoping to find the judges. All I need is to know why they sent for me. Then I can go back to Earth. I far prefer the chaos there to the insanity here.

Someone grabs my arm. I feel my eyes blacken as I turn to face her.

It's the tallest judge. "Come on."

I follow her until we reach the edge of the woods. "I'm not going in there."

She glares at me. "That's where we're meeting."

"That's not where *I'm* meeting."

"Are you for real?" She throws her arms in the air.

I dig my feet into the soil. "You'd better believe it."

Her brows draw together. "We have to discuss strategy."

"Have at it."

"Not out here in the open."

"Then meet me on Earth. I know of plenty safe places where I won't lose four months."

She gives me a dramatic eye roll. "Is that all this is about?"

I don't dignify the question with a response.

"Come *on*."

"No. You can bring in one of my parents as an ambassador if you'd prefer. I'm not going in there."

"You do realize we're in the middle of a civil war, don't you?"

I nod.

"Valhalla as we know it will never be the same again."

I nod again.

"You're being ridiculous."

"I don't have to explain myself to you."

"Actually, you do. I'm the head of the opposition."

"Not if I start my own opposition." I hate it when my mouth runs before clearing it with my brain.

"Excuse me?" Her eyes blacken and her wings explode out, showing a span more than twice of my own.

I draw in a deep breath. "What I mean is, I will deal with the war down on Earth while you handle the one here."

"In case you haven't noticed, that's already what's going on. We can't split the war into two parts. It's one civil war, expanded into two worlds."

"Sounds like we're on the same page. However, you haven't been dealing with valkyrie hunters like I have."

Her eyes fade back to green. "I heard they were eradicated."

"That hasn't been confirmed yet. But the ones who gathered in the battle we just had were all killed. They've been sent to the other side."

"That's what the Earthlings call the place where their dead are taken if we don't get to them first?"

"Yes."

"Can't they just get out again?"

"No. The most powerful witch in the world opened the doors and everyone claims those doors are now permanently sealed. Nobody will ever escape again."

"Including your previous love interest?"

I clench my jaw. She knows about Brick. How much more of my private life do Valhalla's leaders know about? My marriage? Alaska?

"Well?" She arches a brow and brings in her wings.

"Yes."

"I need to update you on what's going on. It's urgent."

"It's all pretty obvious." I gesture toward the nearly-destroyed castle.

"There's more you need to know."

A group of soldiers march our way, calling out a war cry in unison.

The judge squeezes my arm. "Come *on*."

Alaska's face pops into my mind. I shake my head. "Not happening."

"There have been major losses on both sides. You need this information."

"Then tell me here."

"Don't you understand the danger?" She takes a step back, now half in the woods and half out.

The soldiers come closer, their chanting growing louder. One near the middle stops and stares at me. Others crash into her as the ones in front keep going. She points at me, her eyes darkening. "Pregnant valkyrie!"

My blood runs cold.

"Pregnant valkyrie!"

The judge swears, calling down Odin's curses.

All of the soldiers in the line turn to me. They're all chanting, "Pregnant valkyrie!"

The judge turns to me. "Is this true?"

I can't hear her over the soldiers, but I can read her lips easily enough.

I give a small nod.

She mutters something I can't hear or read on her mouth.

All at once, the soldiers lunge for me.

Everything goes black.

CHAPTER TWENTY-ONE

itan

I stare at the food in front of me. Though my stomach rumbles, I can't bring myself to eat. I probably should since I have no idea when Soleil will return. Will she be gone for months again? Longer? I try to push aside my building anger, but it isn't going away.

"You going to eat, Dad?" Alaska looks at me with an expression too young for his teenage face.

"Sorry. Got lost in thought." I pick up the fork and stick something in my mouth so I don't disappoint him.

As I'm halfway through chewing my bite, all the werewolves look up from their plates. Most are looking at the ceiling.

I glance up, not seeing anything, and swallow my food. "What's going on?"

Toby looks at me. "Something just crashed upstairs. Sounds like in one of the bedrooms."

Could it be Soleil? I waste no time leaping from my chair,

knocking it over in the process, and racing up the stairs. "Please be there."

I fling open the bedroom door and look around. The room is empty. I ignore the crushing disappointment and look around the hall, checking each room. Valhalla doesn't always get it right when they send her back.

She's not on the second floor, but I don't let that discourage me. I make my way up to the third floor and check the rooms there. Still nothing.

There's only one more level, unless there's an attic. Then there are two more levels I can check. I hurry up the stairs. "Soleil!"

My stomach twists tighter with each step. The feeling that she's going to be gone for months again is covering me like a heavy blanket. I don't even want to think about the worse alternative— that they discovered her pregnancy and won't let her leave.

I have no way of getting back to her. Not unless one of the valkyries could send themselves there and bring me along. Seems unlikely. Soleil has only ever gone when they've pulled her away from here unwillingly or she's killed her target. But I think that's still them pulling her away. It's all so confusing.

Again, the rooms are all empty. There also isn't an attic I can find. I'll have to ask Toby, though I have little hope that even if they have an attic, she'll actually be there.

I got my hopes up for nothing. She's still in Valhalla, and she's going to be there for a while.

Sighing, I lean against the nearest wall and pull on my hair. There's little I hate more than feeling hopeless, and I've had more than my share of it today. First when Alaska was taking in all that essence and now this.

Why had I been so naive as to think that marrying a valkyrie would be any easier than this? I knew it would have unique challenges, but I never imagined any of this. Who could have foreseen Valhalla falling apart and her leading a faction so soon after marrying? Or any of this with Alaska?

I love them both with everything in me and wouldn't change

that, but this is harder than anything I've ever been through. It's like my heart keeps shattering into a million pieces over and over again. I don't know how to handle this. How to *keep* handling this.

What am I supposed to tell Alaska? How am I supposed to explain this to a boy who looks fourteen, but thinks like a four-year-old and is actually only four months old? I can barely wrap my mind around any of it. How is he supposed to?

"You look like you have the world on your shoulders."

I glance over. Toby. "Two worlds, actually."

He frowns and his forehead creases. "I understand that burden."

"You do?"

"Not the valkyrie world, but the traditional werewolves. Though they lived here, their societies were based on rules that seem out of this world. Rules and traditions that stole Victoria from me for far too many years." His voice cracks. "She died in my arms, you know."

I close my eyes for a moment. "I can't imagine the pain."

"I lived more than a century thinking she'd never return from the other side. But then do you know what happened?"

"It opened up."

He nods. "It did. Like a double-edged sword, it released many. Not only did it free the love of my life, it also released the valkyrie hunters. Many good and evil people alike were let out that day. It brought both heartache and joy. And it wasn't an easy path, even after she stepped back into my life."

"No?"

Toby shakes his head, the pain evident in his eyes. "It was torture. She didn't remember me, our past. Nothing." He draws in a deep breath. "Even though things obviously worked out, I still hate thinking about it."

"Understandable. I can't imagine ever wanting to look back on these days. How did you get through it? If you don't mind answering."

"I don't mind. It—"

"Mom's here!" Alaska's voice drifts from downstairs.

"Tell me that story later." I scramble to the steps and nearly face-plant as my foot slips on one. I grab the railing and steady myself. "Where is she?"

"Here!"

I find Alaska standing in the doorway to our room. "I looked there."

He grabs my arm and drags me in. Points to the other side of the bed.

I didn't look there before.

Soleil is lying on the ground, eyes closed.

"No!" I race over and fall to my knees. "Soleil!"

Alaska and Toby kneel next to her also. Tears shine in Alaska's eyes. "Is she gonna be okay?"

A lump forms in my throat. I nod. "She always is."

Toby puts his hand in front of her nose. "She's breathing, at least. I'm going to find Eveline." He races out of the room.

"Maybe Gessilyn!" I call, not sure if he can hear me.

Alaska takes one of Soleil's hands in both of his. "Wake up, Mom! Wake up, please."

It takes all of my self-control to keep myself from falling apart. Between the two of them, it's more than I can take. I brush some hair from her eyes and kiss her forehead. Then her cheek and her mouth.

"Mom," Alaska begs.

I don't know how much longer I can hold myself together. My pain, I can handle. Alaska's? It'll do me in. No doubt there.

Soleil's eyes flutter.

I jump back and look at Alaska. "Did you see that?"

He nods, his eyes as wide as the full moon.

"Soleil," I whisper. "We're here. Right here."

Her eyelids move again but don't open.

I hold my breath, silently pleading with any unseen force who can help.

"Mom, Mom!" Alaska's practically jumping up and down now.

"Careful. You're bigger now, remember?"

"Oh, yeah." He kneels again. "Mom, please wake up!"

I run my fingers through her hair. "We're right here, Soleil. Alaska and me. We aren't going anywhere. We want you to wake up."

Her eyes flutter, but again, nothing more.

"What happened?"

"Where'd she go?" Alaska asks.

"It's complicated."

"Valhalla?"

I give him a double-take. "You know about Valhalla?"

"Yeah."

"I wish you didn't."

"They don't like me, do they?"

"It's not your fault," I say quickly.

He frowns.

"We love you. That's all that matters. Family is the most important thing, and we have your back. We'll always be here for you. The pack is your family too."

Alaska nods. "They're going to help Mom get better?"

"Right." I hope.

Soleil gasps.

I turn back to her. Her eyes are wide, and her face pales as she looks around.

She's awake! A rush of energy sweeps through me. I wrap my arms around her and kiss her all over her face.

"How'd I get here?"

"I don't know." I keep kissing her. "All that matters is that you *are*."

She struggles to sit up, and I help her. "I don't understand."

"What's not to understand? You're back home."

"I shouldn't be." She shudders.

Alaska throws himself between us and clings to her, nearly knocking us all over. The poor kid really has no concept of his own size. He sobs, soaking her shirt with his tears.

I rub both of their backs. "What happened, Sols?"

"The soldiers attacked me. I never went into the woods."

"Huh?" I try to make sense of it. "What woods? Were they supposed to protect you from the soldiers?"

She shakes her head and sighs. "I refused to go in with the judge because I didn't want to lose more time. Then some soldiers marched by and sensed my pregnancy. They proclaimed it and attacked me. Everything went black. I thought because they hurt me." She glances at her arms and legs. "Doesn't look like they did."

"Could the judge have sent you back here before they reached you?"

"Possibly." She frowns. "It's unlikely. She was torqued that I wouldn't go into the woods to meet with the rest of the opposition. If she wanted me safe, seems like she'd have forced me into the woods."

"Maybe she isn't as bad as she seems?"

"Hard to believe, but it could be." She kisses the top of Alaska's head. "It's okay, sweetie. I'm here."

He looks up, his eyes red. "I don't want you to go away again."

"I don't want to either."

"But you might?" He sniffles.

"Unfortunately. I'm sorry. I don't have any control over that."

The bed scoots away from us. Items on shelves and the desk wobble.

Alaska's eyes widen. "What's going on?"

A framed poster crashes onto the ground and shatters.

"Earthquake!" Soleil shouts.

"Duck and cover!" I leap to protect Alaska, who knows nothing about tremors.

CHAPTER TWENTY-TWO

*S*oleil

The room finally stops shaking. My heart hasn't stopped pounding in my ears. Titan and Alaska are both okay. So am I. We're all safe.

Alaska squirms out from under Titan's protection. "Why was everything shaking?"

"It was an earthquake." I rise and help him to his feet. "Let's make sure everyone else is fine."

Titan stands and dusts himself off. "You two aren't hurt?"

We both say no, then we all head downstairs. Items are strewn across every floor. There are several cracks in the walls on the ground level.

Toby is staring at his tablet. "It's too soon for any news updates, but that had to be at least a seven on the Richter scale."

"It's on the news!" Jet calls from the living room.

We all race over, stepping over fallen objects.

Two newscasters are discussing the quake on the television.

Then the screen pans over to a different room with a man in a lab coat and thick glasses.

"What a nerd," mutters one of the kids.

"No name calling, Wilder." Toby glares at his son.

"Just calling it as it is."

"Shh." Victoria steps closer to Toby and takes his hand. "I want to hear."

The seismologist rambles on, but I can't figure out what he's talking about until he says, "The epicenter was in the heart of Seattle. Our current reading shows it was a nine-point-one."

My mouth drops open. That's catastrophic. Thousands were probably killed. Much of the city would be a pile of rubble, not unlike Valhalla's castle. It's the "big one" they've been talking about for decades.

Unless it was caused by valkyries. Our civil war brought to Earth. Destroying it.

On the screen, everything shakes. The seismologist grabs onto a desk. "Everyone needs to expect aftershocks for some time! Stay safe!"

The screen blackens for a moment before returning to the newsroom.

I step back. "I need to speak with my parents and see if this was because of our war."

Titan and Alaska follow me out of the room. I try unsuccessfully calling both of my parents. Next, I call Gessilyn.

"Are you all okay?" she answers.

"We're fine, are you?"

"Shaken but safe. Whoa!"

I gasp. "Gess!"

"Aftershock. Hold on." After a brief pause, she speaks again. "Just before the earthquake, I was running a locator spell. I have good news."

"Locator spell?" I ask. "For who?"

"Hunters. It came up with nothing. I tried three times. You've officially eradicated them."

I know I should be relieved, but I'm not. Not when we're dealing with earthquakes and a valkyrie war. "Thanks, Gessilyn. I appreciate you looking into that."

"I know it isn't much in the grand scheme of things, but at least that's one less enemy to worry about."

"You're right. Now I can focus solely on the agents of Valhalla." Even though all I want to do is be with my family. Process the fact that one child has aged about fourteen years in four months and we're already expecting another.

"Killian is calling me. I need to take his call."

"Stay safe." I end the call and try my mother again.

She answers this time. "Were you affected by the earthquake?"

"Yeah, but we're safe. Where are you?"

"Most of us are back here in El Salvador. The ground is steady, but there are nearby volcanoes erupting."

"And you're staying there?"

"They aren't even in this country. Any chance you'll be joining us?"

I look at Alaska and Titan. "Not right now."

"You realize that these earthquakes and lava shows all mean one thing, don't you?"

"There are too many valkyries in the area."

"The area? Try the whole Earth. We're offsetting the delicate balance of nature on this fragile planet. And I have reliable intel saying the agents are gathering together. They aren't spread around."

"We need to do something!"

"Right," she snaps. "We need the leader of our faction here with us so we can defeat the enemy."

I close my eyes and take a deep breath. "There are things I need to take care of here."

"Bring them with you."

"You want me to bring my four-month-old son into battle? You're crazy!"

"He's the one who defeated the hunters! And I know that for a fact because a local witch ran a spell and confirmed that they're all dead."

"So did Gessilyn."

"We need a break. Time to recover and rest."

"You think the agents are going to allow that? With everything in disarray, they're going to attack harder than before!"

I bury my face in my hands before responding. "You don't think we can wait one night?"

"Not if we want to win. Time to put on your big-girl britches and face them. Destroy them."

Titan cups my face. "She's right. Let us come with you."

"Alaska too?"

"I think we need him. Just like with the hunters."

I shake my head. "They'll go after him. One whiff of what he is, and he'll be target number one."

Titan leans closer, holding my gaze. "He's stronger than them. Than all of us. Do you think it's a coincidence he was born now? All of this was meant to be. You, me, him."

I press my palms on my stomach. "Baby number two?"

He brushes his lips across mine. "The way things are going now, all of this will be over by the time she arrives. She could be born in a time of peace. We can have our dream of living out the rest of our lives together without the interference of Valhalla—or anyone else, for that matter."

"He's right," my mother says in my ear.

I forgot I was still holding the phone.

I turn my attention from Titan to the phone. "I know you don't have a maternal bone in your body, but how can you agree to this?"

"Because it's the right thing. Even your husband agrees, and we both know how much he cares about you and your son."

I narrow my eyes at Titan. "I can't believe you two are ganging up on me like this."

He gives me an apologetic look. I pull away from him and

speak to my mother. "I'll think about it and get back to you." Then I end the call.

"You'll think about it?"

Before I can respond, the floor shakes. A mirror next to Alaska falls to the ground and breaks.

Titan pulls Alaska away from the glass. "You think this is going to get any better?"

I look at Alaska. "What do you want? Do you want to go back to the dragon castle, where it's safe? Or do you want to go to a foreign country and battle with strong ancient valkyries?"

He frowns. "You always leave when I'm at the castle."

I can't deny that. "But I'll be back. I also always return."

Alaska folds his arms. "I want to stay with you."

Why does this surprise me? "How are you feeling after drinking all that essence?"

"Fine."

"What? You aren't sick at all?"

He shakes his head no.

I take a deep breath. "If we go there, it's going to be dangerous. Probably more than it was outside when the hunters were attacking us."

Alaska stares me down. "I can do it."

I hesitate.

"I know I can." He stands taller. Looks me directly in the eyes.

I turn to Titan, hoping against hope he'll take Alaska somewhere safe.

"I'm staying by your side. And I'm sure everyone here is with me on that." He kisses my cheek.

"Even with all the dead bodies piled up outside? People need time to recover."

Toby walks over. "I didn't mean to eavesdrop, but we're more than happy to help. Your enemies are our enemies."

My stomach churns acid, lurches. Then I realize it's not from nerves. Without a word, I race down the hall to the nearest bathroom and barely make it to the toilet in time to throw up.

Could things get any worse? My son, husband, and pack want to fight the valkyries. The hunters were one thing—tough, yes, but not valkyries. I'm leading the Earthly war on Valhalla, all while pregnant. I really don't see how things could get worse.

As I rinse my mouth, I wrack my mind for reasons to keep everyone else home. But I know better. They're going to want to be at my side, no matter the risk.

I stare at my exhausted reflection and sigh. Hopefully we have enough resources to stand up against Valhalla's agents. But even that might not be enough. None of this will even matter if the opposition fails back there. If that happens, they'll summon the rest of us for the torture yards or execution.

Even if this pregnancy goes as quickly as my first, there isn't time to wait it out and have the baby safely first.

Because of this war, I'm quite literally risking everything—everything I love.

Knock, knock!

"Are you okay, Soleil?"

Titan's voice brings tears to my eyes. I wipe them away but more replace them.

"Soleil?" He knocks again.

I open the door and throw my arms around him. "I don't want to put everyone in danger. We're going to have to face off with valkyries this time, not hunters."

He squeezes me and rubs my back. "We realize the risks, but we want to be here for you. Besides, it's *our* planet they're attacking. Don't you think we have the right to defend it?"

"You have a point."

"I do? I mean, of course I do. I'm just surprised you agree."

I step back, wipe my tears, then look him in the eyes. "I need to convince them to take this back to Valhalla. That way, none of you will have to be affected by this."

He grasps my arms. "That's not what I meant! We want to fight alongside you. All valkyries have the right to decide when they want retirement. Hybrids should be able to walk around free, without worrying they'll be executed. This is bigger than you, bigger than we know. Think of others like Alaska, who live in hiding because they're half-valkyrie. We're fighting for our children, for others like them."

I nod. "You're right. I just don't want to see any unnecessary bloodshed—especially not of our son."

"Have you seen him in action? He took in all that essence and it didn't faze him. We couldn't have beaten the hunters without him."

I frown. "It was close, but we—"

Titan presses his lips on mine. "Stop trying to talk me out of this. You won't be able to. Not me or any of the other supernaturals. The leaders are speaking with others around the world. Vampires, werewolves, witches, dragon shifters, and whatever Tap is—they're all gearing up for this battle on every continent. Oh, and mesmers too. Worldwide, we're going to use every trick in the book to trap those winged agents of death."

My mouth falls open. "Really?"

"Yeah. Those valkyries have no idea what they're up against."

CHAPTER TWENTY-THREE

 itan

We're in a different part of El Salvador than when I was searching for Astrid. This area is run-down and has a sour smell.

Roan leads us down an alleyway with some kind of liquid running down the middle. I try not to breathe through my nose, though it's hard as I'm trying to keep a group of over a hundred supernaturals appearing invisible as we move along.

It's no easy task, and in fact I'm drenched in sweat. That sour stench might be me.

Awesome.

"Here!" Roan opens a door and motions for us to hurry inside.

Soleil gestures for Alaska to go inside first before she rushes past her dad. I race in next, not wanting to let those two out of my sight if I can help it. That's sure to change once the battling begins.

Once inside, I nearly skid to a stop. I've never seen so many valkyries in one place. The sea of blonde hair and blue and green eyes is unlike anything I've ever seen. Alaska is the only one with darker hair, a blend of my golden-brown and Soleil's bright blonde locks. But that isn't what really gets my attention. It's the energy in the air—so much power, I can actually hear a faint buzzing.

After our entire group is inside, Roan closes the door and nods to his wife.

Astrid rises and introduces Soleil to the group. She doesn't mention me or Alaska, probably for our protection. Who knows how many of these valkyries would be against us because of our relationship to Soleil? Many of these ancient angels are likely to hold the same antiquated beliefs as the leaders we're all about to fight.

Soleil fills everyone in on the situation with the hunters—that they've been eradicated—but she leaves out the part about our hybrid son finishing them off. Then she says what she knows about the battles around the world and the earth reacting to the arrival of so many valkyries. "We've experienced some of the earthquakes, while others have dealt with erupting volcanoes or floods, and there are even rumors of darkness in the middle of the day. Can anyone confirm?"

A valkyrie rises. "I can. I arrived on Earth in a busy city in Russia. Everything seemed normal until everything just went dark. Chaos ensued, as you can imagine. I headed straight here."

Soleil nods. "Thank you. All of this proves that more of us are arriving. It's too much for this planet. We need to put an end to this war before both earth and Valhalla are completely destroyed."

Another valkyrie stands. "Should we split up and head to different continents? Divide and conquer?"

Soleil shakes her head. "We need to stick together."

Boom!

The walls shake.

Soleil continues. "More than ever, it's imperative we fight side-by-side. By nature, we're loners. We need to throw that off for now. Once we've won our freedom, we can do what we want. Now, we're an army."

Boom!

The walls shake again, this time a wide crack snakes down one of them.

Soleil takes a deep breath. "They're here. At least some of them. Does everyone have their swords?"

The sea of valkyries pulls out their shiny weapons. Then they discuss battle strategies. Toby pulls the rest of us aside and goes over our part in the war, encouraging all of us to use our own powers as best as we can.

I turn to Alaska. "Are you sure you're up to this?"

He nods, a stark determination in his eyes. "I'm going to protect Mom and my baby sister."

Astrid steps between us and puts a hand on Alaska's shoulder. "I have an important gift for you."

My heart rate triples. I'm not sure I trust her or this supposed gift. "What is it?"

She ignores me and digs into her trench coat. "This is your Valhalla sword." She pulls out a long sword, similar to the ones I've seen every other valkyrie carry, and hands it to him. "I had to sneak back to Valhalla to have it forged—secretly, might I add. Can't talk about my hybrid grandson very easily up there. Anyway, it's just as powerful as any other valkyrie's sword."

My heart thunders even faster. "It won't alert Valhalla of his existence, will it?"

Astrid turns to me. "I'm not stupid."

"I have to ask. Every time Soleil uses hers, she gets yanked away."

"Not *every* time," Astrid corrects. "And even if that were true, all bets are off now. Valhalla's castle is nearly gone. Only one wing remained when I left."

Alaska pulls his sword out of the sheath. "Who's winning up there?"

Astrid frowns. "It's too hard to tell, especially with valkyries coming and going from there to here and back again."

Alaska holds his blade up and studies it. "You sure it's safe for me to use?"

"I wouldn't put you in danger."

Boom!

One of the cracked walls crumbles.

Soleil whistles for everyone's attention. "It's time! Any questions?"

Nobody speaks.

"Good." Soleil looks around the room. "Remember these faces. We're on the same side. We want the same thing—to eradicate the dictatorship in Valhalla. To bring peace to both worlds. If you're fighting for anything else, leave now."

Silence.

She raises her sword. "Go!"

I turn to ask Alaska if he's sure about this, but he's already running outside.

CHAPTER TWENTY-FOUR

 laska

The noise is so loud it hurts my ears. But I barely notice because the harsh sounds send waves of excitement through me. I get to fight in a battle with my parents. To protect my mom.

It hardly seems real. But it is. And the sword in my hands is proof of that.

Valkyries are shouting battle cries all around me. I want to imitate them, but they're so intricate. Similar but different. I don't want to accidentally call out the one from the wrong side.

I'm no bad guy. I'm good, like my parents.

A really muscular valkyrie runs at me, her eyes blackening and her sword glistening. "I know what you are! You must die, hybrid!"

My heart pounds, but instead of feeling the fear I probably should, a strong sense of something brave grows inside me. Pressure builds in my eyes. A shiver runs through me, making me feel like I can do anything.

Maybe I can. Look what I've already done, and everyone seems amazed by that.

The black-eyed valkyrie is almost at me. Her wings are enormous, and her sword is sharp.

I can barely move. Have to remind myself to breathe.

Her sword is coming at me. Right for my heart.

Something near my belly warms and radiates through me. Before I know what's going on, I plunge my sword into her chest. Blood sprays out. Her essence swirls out.

The valkyrie gasps and falls to her knees, calling down curses from Odin. But Odin's gone. Nobody knows where he is. She falls flat on her face. Her sword bounces away. She doesn't move.

My sword warms. Buzzes a little.

"Alaska!" my dad yells.

I spin around in his direction, but before I do, I see another valkyrie lunging at me. Her eyes are just as black as the last one.

My sword almost seems to move on its own. It digs into her and kills her too.

One after another, valkyries come after me. Some of them say they know what I am. Others just want to destroy me.

Not one does. You'd think they would learn, seeing what I do to their friends.

Some of the witches gather around me, saying funny words.

Boom!

Those loud noises keep going off in the distance. I don't know what they are, but it seems like more of the bad valkyries show up with every loud sound.

Now that the witches have stopped speaking, no more valkyries are after me.

I turn to Eveline. "What was that?"

"A spell to keep them from seeing you. It won't last long, though."

"They can't see me?" I exclaim.

She shakes her head. "It'll give you a few minutes to recharge or run. Whatever you want to do."

I know exactly what I want to do. That's an easy choice. I look around for my mom.

She's fighting three bad valkyries.

Eveline starts to say something else, but I don't stick around to find out what. I race over to my mom and swing my sword around, taking out each of the valkyries who can't see me.

Maybe when the spell wears off, I can try to make myself invisible. Dad made all of us invisible, and I have his powers too. I just have to figure out how to use them.

Mom looks at me with big eyes. "How'd you do that?"

I glance Eveline's way. "Magic."

She starts to say something, but then a bad valkyrie runs at her from behind.

"Watch out!"

Mom spins around. Other baddies surround her.

That makes me mad. Really, really mad.

Anger boils inside of me. I focus on that and open my mouth to drink essence. It'll make my mom sad again if I grow more, but at least she'll be alive.

One by one, the valkyries slow. Their heads turn in my direction. One mouth opens, followed by another, then another until they all have essence swirling out from them, heading right for me.

A swirl of essence weaves its way down my throat, then a second, followed by a third. It's a lot. This stuff is stronger than any other essence I've felt. Way more than the guy who kidnapped me and even more than the many hunters who filled me at once.

I hope this doesn't make me into a grownup. That'll really make my parents super sad.

But I have to do this no matter what happens. I'm here for a reason. And maybe that's to help keep my parents and sister safe.

Boom!

Everything lights up orange for a moment. A horrible smell makes me gag. My eyes sting and water, the pressure lessening.

The essences all snap out of my mouth. The bad valkyries aren't dead!

I open my mouth to drink more of their essences, but the yucky odor is too much. I can barely keep my eyes open. They sting!

After I wipe the tears, I manage to keep them open—just in time to see my mom swing her sword at the bad valkyries. Their essences still run through me, but it doesn't feel like much. Not compared to when I drank in all the hunters' essences. Maybe I won't grow fast again.

I hope.

Mom's sword slices through the other valkyries, and they all crash to the ground—dead.

I hurry over to her. "We make a good team!"

"That we do, but try not to drink too much essence."

Boom!

"What is that?" I ask.

She frowns. "Lightning bringing more agents."

"Bad valkyries?"

"Unfortunately."

My stomach flip-flops. "How many are there?"

"It's anyone's guess." She leaps around me, swinging her sword.

I spin around and see five black-eyed valkyries lunging for my mom. Without a thought, I open my mouth and suck in essence. Pressure builds in my eyes, and those bad valkyries turn toward me, mouths open, their essences flying in my direction.

Mom swipes her sword at them, taking out two of them in one solid motion. Their essences snap away from me and I stumble back. Crash into something behind me.

A big group of baddies swarm us. Push between my mom and me. They surround me. I can't see anything other than their faces. The dark eyes.

All essence yanks from me. I open my mouth to drink the essence of those around me.

Dad shouts something from somewhere. I don't know what he's saying. Can't make out any of the words. Not over the valkyries speaking. They're all talking at once. I can't tell what they're saying either.

Something sharp pokes me in the side.

I gasp. See stars. Yell out. Desperately try to drink in more essence.

It doesn't work.

Everything goes black. Something squeezes the sides of my head. Fingers, definitely fingers.

I kick, hit, and yell. My sword drops. Clinks. How can I hear it when I can't hear anything else over all the noise? My grandma is going to be mad I lost the sword since she went all the way to Valhalla to have it made just for me. I open my mouth to drink essence.

A hand presses over my lips, forcing them closed.

I struggle harder. They're dragging me. Pulling me away from my family. Taking me from the only people I know. People who love me, who take care of me.

Maybe I should've listened to my mom when she said I should go back to the dragon castle.

She'll probably be mad at me too.

I fight to get away, but these bad valkyries are super strong. I might be able to fight one of them, but not this whole group. They're taking me farther away from my parents. My sister.

How am I supposed to protect them now?

I bite down on the hand covering my mouth.

A horrible pain radiates through my head. Someone is shouting at me. Saying bad things.

My stomach feels funny. So does my whole body. I'm spinning. Everything is.

Then it stops with a jolt.

All the noise stops. My ears buzz.

I struggle to get free, but the hands continue holding me down. Stronger than me. I could probably stand up to them one at a time, but not like this. Not with them all fighting me at once.

One valkyrie lifts an arm. "Throw him in a cell! We'll deal with this jackanapes once he settles down!"

What's a jackanapes? Me?

Before I can ask, my back and head slam against the ground. More stars. Lots of colors.

I wish my parents were here. But maybe by these bad valkyries taking me here—wherever this is—it's helping them to fight the others.

One of them forces my mouth open. I try to drink in her essence, but she stuffs something awful-tasting into my mouth. It makes me gag. They stick something over my mouth. I'll never be able to spit out the gross thing now.

Someone grabs my arm, squeezes it, then drags me over rocks and other prickly things.

Now I'm flying through the air. I crash into something sharp. It makes a zinging sound. I slam to the hard ground. Roll.

A door slams shut with a resounding clink. It's followed by a *clickety-click* as they lock me in.

I'm in a cell. It's cold in here. The yucky thing in my mouth still tastes so bad. I pull off the sticky thing and spit, then crawl over to the nearest bars and wrap my fingers around them.

Zap!

I back away and shake out my hands.

Nobody is anywhere in sight.

I'm really in trouble.

CHAPTER TWENTY-FIVE

oleil

My mother holds me back as I scream for Alaska. "Focus on the battle at hand!"

"They have him!" Even in my terror, I remember not to refer to him as 'my son.' There's a small chance the other valkyries don't know he's my child—my *hybrid* child.

She turns, still grasping me, and looks into my eyes. "We don't know where they took him. The only chance we have is to beat them now. Think of him as you look at every agent of Valhalla."

A fire burns in my gut as I think of the agents, of what they could do to Alaska.

"Good." Mother nods. "Hold onto that fury. Keep your eyes black. Fight with everything in you. That's what we need if we're going to win and don't want to spend the rest of our lives enslaved or imprisoned. Understand?"

I pull away from her, flapping my wings and clutching my sword. Everything around me comes into a tight focus. I only see the agents of Valhalla. Their hearts are targets. I won't rest until they've all fallen.

Someone calls my name. It sounds miles away, as does everything else from the battle—the screams, clinking swords. Even the thunder bringing more agents.

The more that come here, the more we can eradicate. This is good news. I hold onto the images of Alaska, Titan, and the baby I've yet to see. I'm fighting for them, for our future. For us. And also for all the supernaturals who have joined us in this battle.

I burst into a run and jab my sword into the hearts of as many agents as I can, slowing only to take them out. We're still outnumbered, but the odds are moving closer to our favor. The agents aren't used to fighting vampires, witches, shifters, and the like. It's throwing them off their game. Though the other supernaturals have to work harder—it takes two or more vampires' bites to take down a single valkyrie—they're able to kill them.

Something hard strikes me in the back of the head. The sound echoes, stunning me for a moment. But only a moment. I flap my wings with as much force as they have, knocking someone over, and I spin around, my sword in position to strike.

Two agents stand in front of me, both with black eyes and swords raised high. I swing my sword, and they both block the strike.

Clink! Chink! Clink!

Our blades cry out as we hit with such force that it nearly takes my breath away. I struggle to breathe normally as we perform what appears to be a dance, moving our feet, bodies, and swords with highly calculated moves.

Behind me, someone cries out with the sound of one giving up their life. In front of me, the sky lights up an unnatural shade of blue. Agents scream out their war cry. I release a battle call as I continue to fight the two agents.

Kaja appears beside me and wipes sweat from her forehead. "Need some help?"

I grunt as my sword connects with one of the agents'. "Yeah."

Now that we're fighting two-on-two, the agents have both lost their haughty smirks. Kaja pulls out some bold moves and manages to slice both of our opponents across their faces.

I take advantage of their shock and stab one in the heart. She crumbles to the ground, shouting curses at Kaja and me until her eyes close.

The other agent aims her blade for Kaja, who moves but not quickly enough. It tears through her sleeve, and red soaks the fabric. I dig my sword into the agent's chest. She drops her weapon and clutches her wound. Color drains from her face. She opens her mouth, and I prepare for a battle of essence, but her eyes close and she falls on top of her friend.

I turn to congratulate Kaja, but I freeze before a word escapes my lips. Her eyes widen and her arms go limp, though she doesn't fall. Blood drips from the corners of her mouth. Her weapon drops just as the end of another sword sticks out through her chest, dripping red.

It takes me a moment to recover from the shock as her eyes start to roll back.

"No!" I reach for her.

The blade disappears from her chest and she starts to fall. I race over and catch her before she crashes to the ground. I help her lie down, ready to fight the agent who did this, but she's already fighting someone else.

"I'll avenge you!" I promise.

"Just... defeat... them."

"We will. And I'm going to make that valkyrie pay."

"Thanks for everything." Kaja's words are garbled. "Without you, I'd still be in that cell. At least I got to experience life down here."

Her eyes close.

"Kaja!"

Her head rolls back.

I check her breathing.

Nothing.

She barely got to live!

There's only one thing to do. I carefully lay her head on the ground before leaping to my feet and jumping over bodies until her killer is only inches from me.

"This is for Kaja!"

The agent turns to me, fire in her eyes. I extinguish it by removing her head. Then I dig my blade into every agent I see. They want to play dirty with backstabbing, I'll play. I aim for just above the middle of the wings whenever possible and sword fight the rest.

As we fight, the sky darkens, and we battle in the dark. Everyone can see well enough that it doesn't slow down either side. The vampires and werewolves seem to have the best sight and take down more agents than the rest of us combined, then our side finally starts to gain the advantage.

By the time the sun lights the sky again, we greatly outnumber them. Both sides have suffered losses, but we now have the upper hand. We're all exhausted and hungry. At least I am, and I assume the others have to be as well. This would be a great time for Laura to show up with heaps of food.

Unfortunately, that won't happen. She's at home with the pack kids.

I should've had Alaska stay with her. Should have fought for it. Now he's with agents, suffering who-knows-what.

Titan stumbles over to me, dried blood caked to his hair and clothes. "It's finally starting to look promising."

I frown. He doesn't know about Alaska.

"What?"

"Alaska..." I struggle to find the words. Can't bring myself to tell Titan that he's been kidnapped. *Again.*

He nods, pain evident in his expression. "I heard. I've killed more agents since then. They *will* pay."

"I don't even know where to start looking. They might be trying to lure me back to Valhalla."

An agent runs our way behind Titan, her sword aimed for his back.

I jump around him and swing my blade so hard against hers that she lets go. It flies through the air and the handle crashes into a wolf before falling to the ground. Her face contorts in anger, but before she has a chance to say anything, I dig my weapon into her chest with such force that when I yank it out, it brings her heart along with it. She crashes to the ground and I swing the sword so her organ comes loose.

"Thanks." Titan steps aside.

I wipe my blade on my pants. "Nobody goes after you and lives. Not on my watch."

He starts to say something, then stops. His eyes narrow, appearing to be focused on something behind me. He maneuvers around me and plunges his knife into the neck of an agent before turning to me. "I have your back too, babe."

We stand back-to-back and fight off agents that way until the sky starts to go dark again. Another day gone, another day spent in battle.

A day that our son has been missing, taken captive by agents who will want him dead if they figure out what he is. Agents who will be eager to throw me into the torture yards once they discover what I've done—married a mesmer, had a hybrid offspring, and have another on the way.

A horn sounds not far away. It plays a tune I learned thousands of years ago in valkyrie school.

It can only mean one thing.

CHAPTER TWENTY-SIX

itan

I crumble to the ground and cover my ears, not that it does any good against the high-pitched horn blaring. It feels like my eardrums are going to explode, followed by the rest of my body. I don't know what that horn is, but it's not from this world. Terror grips me as I try to guess what will happen next.

Soleil flings herself on me, blocking the noise. My ears ring in the absence of the blaring assault.

I gasp for air and take in the relief of the quiet before nudging her off. She rolls off and pulls some hair away from her eyes. Even though she's not blocking the sound, it's gone.

"What was that?" I sit up and rub my ears.

"They've retreated."

I give her a double-take.

"We won this battle. Those still standing fled back to Valhalla." She jumps to her feet and offers me her hand.

I take it and she pulls me up. "So, they're really gone? For now, at least?"

She nods, and we both look around. The ground is littered with bodies, and other valkyries from our side are speaking with the remaining supernaturals. I try to find everyone we know but it's too dark and everyone is too spread out.

Soleil whistles and calls everyone over. She waits until everyone has gathered before speaking. "Though it doesn't feel like it, this has been a victory. Agents of Valhalla have retreated! That horn you heard was their version of walking away with their tails between their legs."

The valkyries all raise their swords and say something in Norwegian. The rest of us raise our weapons, though nobody says anything. I get the feeling everyone else feels like me—this is hardly a win.

Soleil continues. "Let's have a moment of silence for the fallen after we list them off. Starting with Kaja."

My stomach knots at hearing the name of the young valkyrie who Soleil mentored for a short time. Everyone else calls out names. A lot of names. I recognize some of the younger members of Toby's pack. None of the species is left without listing off a few of their own, even the mesmers. I didn't know most of the dead, but my heart aches for them nonetheless.

I glance at Soleil, not sure if we should say anything about Alaska. He's been taken captive, but I have to hold onto the hope that he's still alive. He has to be. I can't cope with any other outcome.

After the last name is spoken, we stand silently for a minute before Soleil speaks again. "This is far from over. Not only have they kidnapped one of our own, but there are battles just like this still raging all over the globe. The agents of Valhalla won't stop until we've been defeated. We can take some time to rest and recover, but we need to hit them hard. At lunchtime tomorrow, we reconvene back at the werewolves' property." She makes eye contact with each valkyrie and they nod, then she looks at everyone else. "Obviously, you aren't required to do anything. We appreciate your help more than you know, and I implore you to seek out more help and return with us at noon tomorrow. This war affects not only valkyries, but everyone on this planet. If the agents return with more numbers, there will be more erupting volcanoes, more earthquakes, more tsunamis, and more natural disasters of every kind—perhaps even some we've never seen before."

Astrid steps up and gives updates of other battles across the planet and in Valhalla. My mind wanders back to Alaska, making it hard to focus. I'd be going crazy if I hadn't seen him finish off the hunters on his own. If I hadn't seen him singlehandedly kill his first kidnapper. The only thing I don't like about these memories is the fact that he ages each time. He could come back to us as a full-grown man with the mind of a small child.

But at least he'd be with us. We could still raise him—hide our little family away somewhere until his mind grows into his body. It would be possible.

If we can find him. Or he finds us.

Soleil takes my hand. "Are you ready?"

I shake my head to bring myself back to the present. "Sorry, what?"

"We're all heading home to rest for a few hours."

"Right. By home, do you mean the mansion? The dragon castle? Australia?"

"I think if Alaska came looking for us, he'd go to the mansion."

"Probably."

"Close your eyes."

"Wait!" I pull away from her. "Do you have enough essence to teleport both of us?"

She nods. "I've had to drink several powerful agents dry. I'll feel better after this, I swear."

"Okay." I close my eyes.

Soleil puts a hand on my back and leans against me. I hardly feel a thing before I smell stew and biscuits. I open my eyes, and sure enough, we're already in the mansion. In the living room, more specifically.

"Are you all back?" Laura calls.

"Briefly," Soleil replies.

Crash!

Several pack members appear with one of Gessilyn's sisters next to a mirror. Then another group of werewolves appear with Gessilyn. A crash sounds upstairs, then another down the hall.

"Dinner's ready!" Laura announces. "Wasn't sure when everyone'd be back, so I've kept it simmering!"

I pull Soleil into my arms and squeeze. "Are you okay?"

"As okay as I can be. Are you?"

"Yeah. Where do you think they took Alaska?"

"Could be Valhalla, or it could be somewhere here. I don't know what their intentions are."

My stomach knots. "He should be here with us."

She nods. "But nothing is as it should be."

I start to say something but stop when Astrid comes over. "Roan is going to a few key valkyrie locations to see if Alaska is being held in any of them. I've sent word for others to keep a lookout."

Soleil grits her teeth. "And if he's in Valhalla?"

Astrid hesitates. "Then we have a whole different set of problems."

"What will we do then?" I demand.

Astrid turns to me. "Whatever we can. The fact that they didn't also take Soleil makes me think he's still here."

"Why's that?"

Soleil swallows. "Because they'd want to execute the both of us together. Him for what he is, and me for allowing him to be born."

Anger pulsates through me. "And what about me? I play a part in all of this."

Soleil nods. "But they wouldn't care. I'm the valkyrie responsible for an illegal hybrid."

"That's just wrong."

"That's why we're fighting them. It's the only way for both Alaska and me to be truly free."

Laura pokes her head in. "Come and eat. I know you have to be hungry after such a long battle."

We reluctantly follow her and take a seat at the large table, surrounded by ravenous werewolves. I pick at my food, hardly able to think about anything other than Alaska. My eyelids grow heavy, but I fight them.

"Come on." Soleil rests a hand on my knee. "Let's get some sleep. We're going to have to join a battle tomorrow. There's one raging near St. Louis, and the opposition there needs our help."

I take a deep breath, every bone and muscle in my body aching. "And what about finding Alaska?"

"Gessilyn's running a locator spell as we speak."

I frown. "But if he's in Valhalla, she won't find squat."

"Like my mother said, they're not likely to take him without me."

I clench my jaw. "Then they're using him as bait to get you. I'll go after him once Gessilyn figures out where he is."

She kisses my cheek. "Let's sleep on it."

Sleep on it. Right. "Sure thing."

We head upstairs and change out of our bloody, torn clothes. I urge Soleil to take the first shower, and when she does, I find Gessilyn in a guest bedroom running a spell. Not wanting to interrupt, I sit across from her on the other side of the map with spinning gems.

She opens one eye. "I'm looking for someone else right now."

My heart sinks.

"But I did pick up Alaska's trail."

My breath hitches. "Where?"

"Missouri."

I give her a double-take. "Near St. Louis?"

Gessilyn tilts her head. "How'd you know?"

"Soleil mentioned a battle there where our help is needed."

"Interesting. I'd definitely follow up on that if I were you."

"Were you able to pick anything else up about Alaska? Is he okay?"

"He's alive and on this planet. That's as much as I know. To find out more, you're going to have to find him."

My heart races. "Can you find a more specific location? Near St. Louis is fairly vague. Not that I don't appreciate you telling us that much. I do. But I need to know more. This is my son we're talking about."

"Once we get there tomorrow, I can work on it. For now, get some sleep. You look like death warmed over. With some rest, you'll stand a much better chance of not only finding him, but getting him back."

I hate to admit she's right. "I think they're using him as bait to get Soleil. Any way you can keep this from her? To keep her safe."

Soleil appears in the doorway, wearing a fluffy purple bathrobe and with a green towel on her head. "Keep what from me?"

I groan. "Nothing."

"Keep what from me?" she repeats.

"You're too curious for your own good." I rise and give her a quick kiss, then throw Gessilyn a pleading look.

Soleil cups my chin. "I still find it adorable when you try to protect me. Now go get your shower while I talk to Gess." She shoves me toward the hall and pats my backside. "Hurry up. I have a feeling we're going to find Alaska tomorrow."

"It's you they want, Sols. Let me do this."

"We're in this together, right?"

I frown.

"Go. We both need sleep. And there isn't much time left."

"Okay." I throw Gessilyn another pleading expression, but I can tell Soleil will get her way.

CHAPTER TWENTY-SEVEN

oleil

My phone's ringtone wakes me. I feel like I haven't gotten a wink of sleep.

"You gonna get that?" Titan asks.

I groan and feel around the nightstand until I find the blasted thing and accept the call without looking to see who it is. "Hello?"

"Are you still sleeping?" It's my mother.

"What do you mean *still*? I just fell asleep."

"You're going to have to drink some essence. Things have taken a turn for the worse here in St. Louis."

I sit up. "You're already there?"

"What's going on?" Titan mumbles and rolls over toward me.

"Just tell your pack friends to hurry!" The call ends.

"What is it?"

I stare at my phone for a moment. "Something's going on in St. Louis."

"It's not Alaska, is it?" Titan sits up.

"I don't think so. Sounds like the battle isn't going so well over there."

"We'd better go!" He flings off the covers and rifles through his clothes in the closet.

I force myself up and find some clothes, my mind racing. We quickly get dressed, then rush out and tell Toby what's going on.

"I'll let the other packs know, then we'll head over." He squeezes my arm. "We'll win this and find Alaska. I promise."

"Thanks, Toby."

Ziamara rounds the corner. "Do you want to drink my essence? You always say mine has extra strength."

I hesitate, but she's right. Vampire essence is especially powerful for some reason. "Are you sure?"

She stands taller. "I'm offering, aren't I?"

"Take her up on it," Titan urges.

"Okay. Thanks." I quickly drink some of her essence, finally feeling awake and invigorated. Then I teleport Titan and me to St. Louis.

We aren't anywhere near the battle. I cup my ears, trying to hear war cries or swords clinging, or something.

Nothing.

Twenty minutes and several phone conversations with my mother later, Titan and I find the place. I recognize several of the valkyries who fled our battle in El Salvador.

"What do you think?" Titan squeezes my hand as we take in the scene before us.

I take a deep breath and size up the situation. "I'd say our side is outnumbered three-to-one."

He grimaces. "That's worse than yesterday."

"Right."

"And the others are coming?"

"They'd better be." I text back and forth between both Toby and my mother before answering Titan. "Gessilyn's family is getting ready to bring the werewolves here, the vampires are traveling through the dragon tunnels, and everyone else is finding various ways to get here. The local werewolves are preparing themselves. Once everyone is here, we should hopefully be equal in number to the agents."

He nods. "To be honest, I just want to find Alaska. I can't stop thinking about what he must be going through."

"Me too." I take a deep breath. "Gessilyn said she'll work on that once she gets here. Let's get in there and kill as many agents as we can."

Titan glances at my stomach. "You sure you're up for this?"

I press my palm on my nearly-flat belly. "I have to do this before I'm *obviously* pregnant. They'll haul me away for sure then."

He starts to say something, but I don't want to debate this. I was fine yesterday, and I'm going to be fine today too. Before running into the battle, I give him a quick kiss then ready my sword. Right now, all of this is for my family. They've dragged my son away, and my pack has taken hits but are still willing to help with this battle here. This better be it. I don't know if I have it in me to teleport somewhere else and pick up again.

I dash toward the nearest valkyrie on the traditional side. My stomach clenches. Despite the war, it feels wrong to kill another of my kind. We aren't meant to be against one another. Yet here we are, killing each other in massive numbers.

Keeping Alaska's face in my mind, I plunge my blade into the Valkyrie's back, right between her wings. She lets out a horrifying cry as her essence escapes, then she crumples to the ground.

I recognize the valkyrie she'd been fighting from the meetings with my mom. She pulls some hair from her eyes and takes a raspy breath. "Thanks. She was a lot stronger than me."

"No problem. Need some essence?"

She studies me. "Something's different about your essence."

My heart sinks. She doesn't sense my pregnancy, does she?

"Vampires?" she asks.

My knees nearly give out. I try to hide my relief. "Right, yeah. I filled up on vampire essence before heading over."

"Oh, weird. Okay. No, I'll—"

Three valkyries charge us, all bearing their swords. My new friend and I press against each other and fight as one, eventually taking them down.

Sweat drips down my face, and I gasp for air as I look around. "Have they multiplied?"

She wipes blood from her blade onto her pants. "Maybe. Should be true for our side, as well. I keep hearing reports of battles finishing in other places around the planet. The surviving valkyries are heading to other battle locations."

"I haven't been here very long, but it already looks like there are at least a third more." I squint, studying a group in the distance. Some of the warriors are biting the necks of traditional valkyries. "The vampires are here."

My friend shudders. "How can you stand to be around those creatures of the night?"

"They're on our side." I jump around her and stab a valkyrie headed our way. "I'm going to join them."

"Good luck with that." She turns to help a valkyrie fighting off two others.

I glance around, hoping to see Titan. It's too hard to make out an individual face, given all the wings, clinking swords, and shouting. As I dart through the crowd, heading for the vampires, I help other valkyries along the way.

When I reach the vampires, my mouth drops open. The king and queen are battling, but not like I'd have expected. They're in the air, surrounded by some kind of bubble, using a type of electric power. I've never seen anything like it.

As I stare, something hits me in the side. It takes me a moment to recover, to realize I'm being attacked. I nearly drop my sword, but cling to the handle before it falls. Then I spin around, aiming the blade for my attacker. She puts up a hand, and the tip of my weapon goes through it. As she cries out, I finish her off, then I run toward a vampire I recognize from Italy.

"What's up with the king and queen? Literally." I glance up, where they're still fighting valkyries above our heads.

"It's a long story." He leaps around me and digs his fangs into a valkyrie right behind me.

The fighting goes on for hours, and my eyelids grow heavy. My sword even weightier.

A hand rests on my shoulder. I whip around slowly.

It's Toby.

Relief washes through me.

Concern fills his eyes. "You're so pale. Have you been injured?"

I rub a gash in my arm. "It's not from this. I'm low on essence, plus..."

He nods knowingly. "Take some of my essence. I'm not a vampire, but it has to be better than nothing."

"I can't. You need your strength—you're leading all the werewolves."

"You don't need to remind me. I'm fine, but you aren't."

My aching muscles and inflamed skin agree.

"Come on." He pulls me along a path where surprisingly, nobody is fighting. "Quick. Take my essence."

"I shouldn't."

"Doesn't Alaska need you strong? And..." His voice trails off as he glances at my stomach then back to me.

He's right, and I can't deny it.

"Hurry!" Toby opens his mouth, as if that'll help extract his essence.

Lightning bolts flash across the sky. Valkyries fly down toward us.

I close my eyes and pull Toby's essence, drinking it as quickly as I can without hurting him. As it weaves down my throat and through me, it massages my aches and pains. I'm filled with strength and renewed energy. Then I cut off the flow and open my eyes. "Thank you."

He shakes his head, with a dazed look in his eyes. "I always forget how strangely pleasant that is."

"It—"

His eyes widen. "Watch out!"

I spin but he's already leaping around me, swinging a long knife at a group of five valkyries. They pile on top of him.

"No!" Terror grips me. I can't let anything happen to him.

There isn't time to use my sword. I open my mouth and prepare for the swell of essence I'm about to receive from these strong valkyries. There's a reason I haven't made a habit of drinking other valkyries' essences when fighting.

I'll have to deal with those consequences later. The essences of five powerful valkyries swirl toward me and hit me like a punch to the face. I stumble back, trying to ground my feet. The valkyries all lift off Toby and hang in the air, held in place by their outflowing essence.

Someone shoves me. Hard.

I fly through the air, losing my grip on the essences. My hands instinctively cover my belly to protect the baby.

CHAPTER TWENTY-EIGHT

itan

I wrap my arm around Soleil and do everything I can to steady myself as we fly through the air. My only goal is to keep her safe. Hopefully, I got to her before she inhaled too much essence.

We crash into a tree, but I take the brunt of it. My shoulder slams against the massive trunk, and my head hits with a sickening thud. But she's okay. She didn't hit, and she doesn't have any more valkyrie essence flowing into her.

"Titan?" Her eyes widen with surprise. "What was that all about?"

I rub my head. "That's what I should be asking you."

"What do you mean? I was saving Toby. Those valkyries were—"

"You can't take in all that essence! Not now."

"I wouldn't do anything to put the baby at risk. Hopefully you know that."

I take a deep breath. "We don't *know* what that much essence could do. Better safe than sorry."

"It could help the baby. We valkyries need essence."

"But too much of it can hurt you. Do I really need to remind you?" I dust off my clothes and try to ignore the ringing in my ears.

A bright light shines in the sky, nearly blinding me. Ears still ringing, I jump in front of Soleil to protect her. But I can't see anything, can't open my eyes, so there isn't much I can do beyond shielding her.

She gasps. Shakes. Breathes raggedly.

I turn to look at her. Still can't open my eyes. "What is it?"

Soleil stumbles over her words. Shakes harder.

My heart thunders in my chest. "What?"

"Not what. Who."

"Who?" I demand.

If she responds, I can't hear her over the eruption of shouts and screams.

Even with my eyes closed, I can tell the light is growing brighter. I have to cover my already-closed eyes, but it does little to help.

"Flee!" Gessilyn shouts. "All non-valkyries have to get out of here!"

I turn my head to where I think Soleil's eyes are. "Let's go!"

"All non-valkyries. Go!" She shoves me.

"Not without you!"

"It's Odin!"

"I thought he—"

"He's here. You have to go! Now!" She pushes me again.

Someone grabs my arm. Drags me away. I try to fight, but can't. Not against the bright light. It feels like it's melting me. Once the pain eases, I yank my arm away and run on my own, still unable to open my eyes. Running blind. It'll be a miracle if I don't crash into something.

Feels like I've run through the entire state before the light dims. How I haven't further injured myself, I don't know. Seems impossible.

I crack open one eye. The light doesn't hurt. I crack open the other eye. Still doesn't hurt. I take a deep breath and look around, eyes wide.

Gessilyn and her family all have their palms out. A shimmery film surrounds the group of us non-valkyries who are running. Jet runs into a tree, but goes right through it. Unharmed—both him and the tree.

After I get over my shock, I yell, "The light is safe now!"

In a massive blur of confusion, people stop running while others continue on. Everyone talks at once, and I can't hear a thing. I skid to a stop as I go through a boulder and come out in one piece on the other side.

Toby whistles so loud, I swear my head will explode. I cover my ears, and the tone is worse than it was before. At least I can still hear, even if it is only the ringing.

Once the alpha pulls his fingers from his mouth, I uncover my ears. They're still buzzing but at least the whistle isn't an assault anymore.

Toby speaks, and I can actually hear him. "We can't be in the presence of Odin. It's too much for us, as we all just experienced. But we need to figure out another way to help with this."

"It's not our battle. I'm done!" A werewolf I don't recognize throws his hat on the ground. "It's not worth it. I just watched my best friend lose an arm!"

Toby nods. "I'm truly sorry about your friend. We've all experienced losses since the Valhalla civil war has come here. Some of my young pack members are gone. But whether or not any of you care about valkyries or Valhalla, this affects us all. If too many of them arrive here, they *will* destroy our planet! You just saw what happened when Odin arrived. My understanding is there are eleven others, nearly as powerful as he is. Imagine if they show up! Twelve of that!"

Everyone speaks over each other again. My mind races, trying to figure it all out. Odin times twelve would be devastating.

Toby brings his fingers to his mouth, and I cover my ears before he destroys my eardrums.

When he pulls his hand away and starts talking, I listen again.

"This is unlike anything we've ever seen. If we want to live to see tomorrow, we have to stick together and fight even harder than before."

"What about the dragon cities?"

"Can't the witches protect us?"

"How do we defeat them?"

"Maybe we should just give up and say goodbye to our loved ones!"

So many others shout that I can't make out what anyone says.

I lean against the boulder, but it won't support me. I fall to the ground right in the middle of it, then jump back to my feet.

After everyone calms down, Toby can finally talk again. It takes too long, but everyone finally agrees to head for a nearby building and find out what's going on in the other valkyrie-hit areas. We travel a little farther, continuing to go through objects until we reach a farmhouse that one of the local werewolves claims to own.

I hope he's right. Once the witches drop their forcefield, we're exposed again.

One of the vampires turns to Gessilyn. "Why didn't you use that on us during the battle?"

She wipes some sweat from her forehead. "Because it takes a lot out of us, and I also don't have a complete grasp over it since I've only recently learned the spell."

I put a hand on her arm. "Are you okay? You look a little pale."

She nods. "Even with my family's help, protecting this many people with that spell takes a lot out of me."

"Do you need anything? I'd offer essence or even blood, but I don't think that'd help."

Several vampires turn my way at the mention of blood.

"The offer is for her only," I clarify.

Toby calls everyone inside and we all sit around the living room and start making calls. Pretty much everyone I know is either here or fighting Odin. The thought of Soleil being there gives me the chills. The thought of still not knowing where Alaska is breaks my heart.

I call my parents to find out what they know.

My dad answers and doesn't know much. "Your mom is ill, so we're staying home. I'm using trickery to keep everyone away. Some of your siblings are out fighting valkyries in the area. Haven't heard from anyone."

"Has there been a really bright light? As in, an insanely blinding light?"

"No. Sorry."

"Thanks, anyway. Tell Mom I hope she feels better soon."

"To be honest, I'm glad she's sick."

"Dad, that's horrible!"

"All I mean is, I don't think we're up to battling at our age. I think she's stopped having kids, son. It's been a couple of years."

That's definitely the main sign of aging for our kind, and I hate to think of my parents that way, but they've been around more centuries than me. "Tell her once this is all over, I'm coming to visit. Me, my wife, and kids."

"Kids?"

I curse myself for the slip of the tongue. "You know what I mean. I gotta go. Have valkyrie to fight."

"Actually, I don't know what you mean."

"Bye, Dad." I end the call before I have to get into it.

Toby calls everyone to order and asks what people have found out. The consensus is that battles are still going on around the globe, but the number seems to be dwindling. It's too hard to say which side is winning at this point. However, there haven't been any new reports of natural disasters.

"Nobody else has heard anything about Odin's equals showing up anywhere else?" Toby asks.

A murmured, "No," followed by a chorus of them runs through the room.

Toby nods. "Good. That means it's limited to here. Anyone available should join us. We're going to need all the help we can get."

CHAPTER TWENTY-NINE

laska

I just need to get past those bars. Those ouchy bars. I've been staring at them since I got here—there isn't anything else to do—and I think I can break their energy.

But I have to make sure nobody else is looking. Someone already got mad at me and grabbed my arm, pulling me against those zappy bars.

Just thinking about it makes me rub my skin. These people are all mean, and I have to get back to my parents. They needed me for the hunters, and they need me for this. I can beat valkyries, I just know it. I can feel it.

The problem is these bars. They don't fully stop my powers, but I can't make my powers go past them. That makes me think I could try to use my powers on the bars and break them to get out. But the mean people would notice, for sure.

That gives me more problems. Maybe something worse than the bars.

There have been whispers about someone named Odin. Maybe he can help me. But first, I have to help myself. And for now, I don't dare try. Not with so many people coming and going.

It's getting dark again. Maybe I can work on the bars later. People usually disappear after nightfall. Maybe I can break the bars' power and get away without anybody noticing. Hopefully I'm that lucky.

I'm not sure I am. These people are mean, and they want to keep me here.

Maybe they're afraid of me. What if that's it? They might just be trying to keep me from my family, but what if they *are* scared of my powers? They couldn't beat the hunters.

I did. Not by myself, but I went out there to help Mom and Dad and the werewolves. And I did it. The bad guys lost. I grew again.

Worry runs through me. What if I fix this, but then grow more? Mom and Dad will be sad again. They don't like it when I grow fast. I don't really like it either, but it only happens when I beat the bad guys.

And I need to again. My parents have to be so worried. How can they fight and worry at the same time? I need to show them I'm okay. Once they see me, we can all battle together. I'm brave. I can do this!

I sit up straight and look around while pretending to look at my hands. I'm really looking past them and past the ouchy bars to see what's going on beyond.

There aren't many people. When I first got here, there were a lot of valkyries, but I haven't seen as many since the last sun up. Maybe they're out fighting or something. But they can't be on the good side—not when they took me from my family.

Anger burns inside me. It feels like a thunderstorm, making me shake. Makes my skin hot. Makes me want to rip the zappy bars out from the floor and ceiling of this cage. I want to scream.

Instead, I just let the feeling run through me. If I have enough of it, I think I can ruin the bars. Get away and help my parents.

The darkness overtakes the light until all I can really see is the energy from the buzzing bars. Nobody's paying any attention to me. In fact, I can't see anyone at all.

Maybe this is my chance.

I hold my breath. If I wait, someone might return. Then I can't go through with my plan.

I'm going to have to act now. No other choice.

My heart thunders, making my whole body shake. It's hard to breathe. Hard to focus on my anger.

But I have to. No other choice. This is my chance.

I take a deep breath and hold onto the thought of my parents. The baby sister I want to meet.

This is for them.

My anger swirls around inside me again. I narrow my eyes and glare at the bars. The bad, bad bars. They hurt me before, and now I'm going to break them. They'll never hurt me again if I have anything to say about it.

I release my breath and look around outside the bars. It's harder to see in the dark, but not impossible. I still don't see anyone.

It's time!

I'm not sure how I'm going to do this, but I have some ideas. The first is what has already worked for me before. I open my mouth and suck in, hoping to pull the zappiness right out of them. Maybe it works like essence.

There's only one way to find out. I keep pulling for essence. The bars don't seem to change. I try harder.

Essence from someone else swirls my way from outside my cage. Maybe that'll help me do what I need to do.

The essence weaves its way between two of the bars and enters my mouth. It swirls down into my throat and down to my tummy. It's comforting and sweet. Images fill my mind. Someone else's life. Another person here against her will. I see her cage. It's like mine.

I close my mouth and cut off the flow. If I keep this up, she'll die. I can't kill a good person, and I can see her memories. She's good.

There has to be another way to beat the bars' power. I just have to find it. If only I knew how.

Energy buzzes around in me from the essence. It mixes with my anger like a dance. I still have essence in me from before.

I have enough to spew it out and still have energy left for myself. Maybe I can knock the power out of the bars that way.

My heart pounds again. I clench my fists and focus on breaking down the bars. I only need to take out two. I could fit past those to get out. That's all I need.

If I can do this. No. Not *if*. I *can* do this.

I let myself be angry again and focus on two side bars. I stare at them until my head starts to hurt. The essence runs around inside me, crazier than a storm.

My mouth opens by itself. Essence races up my throat. I hope this works. It flies out of my mouth and crashes into the bars I want to break. It circles around, moving up and down. Sparks fly out from the bars. They sizzle and hiss. They light up, then darken.

Crack! Crack!

I jump back and bump into an ouchy bar behind me. Then I leap forward, continuing to send essence to the dying bars.

The essence stops going around the bar. It heads away from them, away from the cage.

I close my mouth, and it snaps back to me.

The two bars are black and peeling. Cracked. They look like they could break if I touch them.

My mouth goes dry. I have to see if it'll work. My hands are shaking, but I reach for the bars. I touch one.

It crumbles, turning to dust.

I gasp, hardly able to believe my eyes.

Then I poke the next one. It does the same thing. Now there's a big, gaping hole. Just enough space for me to fit through.

I look around, afraid I'll get in trouble, but nobody is around. Nobody knows what I've done.

My knees knock together as I step toward the gap. Ashes crunch under my feet. I turn sideways and slide between the still-bad bars. It's a tight fit, but I manage to get through without hurting myself.

I glance around again. Still nobody. I creep down the tight path between two zappy cages and step out to freedom. My knees are still shaking. It's not just because I was scared.

I've made myself run low on essence. I need more if I'm going to get away and find my family.

I can do this. I have to. No other choice. I'll just have to be super careful.

The question is, where to get it? Here? Or wait until I'm away from the bad guys who brought me here? I kind of want to take their essence—all of it.

The more I think about that, the more I like the idea. They took me from my family, so they should refill me. I want them so low, they can't do anything to me or anyone else.

I stand tall. That's what I'll do. Take their essence then get outta here. Maybe teleport myself back to the battle.

Everything is so quiet. I can't tell where anyone is. I'll have to sneak around until I find someone. I wish they hadn't taken my weapon. But really, it doesn't matter. I'm my own weapon!

I tiptoe to the right and pass more cages. I've seen a lot of people head this way, so there has to be something useful. Hopefully a building, then I can stand outside and drink as much essence as I want from the people inside.

Afterward, I can get back to the battle. If I'm going to have to drink essence there, I have to be careful not to take in too much here. Just enough to get myself back and slow these bad guys down.

The dirt path winds up and down and around trees. Maybe I'm going the wrong way. Could be something scary up ahead. Maybe a trap.

I stop in my tracks and look around, but see little. It's too dark. I close my eyes and focus on all my other senses. The hairs on the back of my neck don't stand up like other times I've been in danger. This could be good.

Crunch!

I spin around, my head feeling like it'll explode. It doesn't.

Five valkyries stand before me, all holding their swords.

Terror sweeps through me. I freeze. My feet won't move.

They're going to capture me. Make me pay for escaping.

But they're not coming after me. They're staring at me, and they kind of look scared.

Of me.

One of them drops her sword. Two others exchange worried glances.

What's going on?

Another kneels. "Odin, you're majesty."

The others fall to their knees. "All hail Odin!"

They think I'm Odin? *Why* do they think I'm Odin?

"How can we serve you, mighty Odin?"

I swallow. "Give me your essence."

They all open their mouths.

Is this real, or a trick?

There's no time to worry about it. I have five valkyries willing to feed me their essence. I open my mouth and hope they aren't about to trap me.

CHAPTER THIRTY

Soleil

I gasp for air and no sooner fly backward as another gust of essence slams into me. That stuff is flying all over the place. It's harder to fight with Odin here.

That's putting it mildly.

And the crazy thing is, I can't tell whose side he's fighting. Seems to be fighting everyone.

I just want to live. To stay on earth. Have my family. Protect my loved ones. I'm glad they all left after Odin showed up. Hopefully they sensed how powerful he is and won't be back. I don't want them to find Alaska.

My head hits the tree first, then the rest of my body. I slide to the ground, gasping for air. Stars dance before my eyes. I rise and shake my head, but my vision is still blurred by the white dots.

I take several deep breaths, and the view becomes clear. Never have I seen so many downed valkyries in one place. The fighting has been going on for days. Days. I've lost count of how many times the sun has disappeared and risen again.

I'm not sure how much longer I can keep this up. How much longer I can continue fighting.

The ground shakes. For a moment, I'm not sure if it's me, but then an ear-shattering crack sounds just before the ground splits in two. It leaves a gap of about a foot zigzagging down the middle of the battlefield.

I press my palm against the tree. Most of the others lift into the air and continue fighting.

That's when I realize nobody notices I'm off to the side. I could walk away, and none of the other valkyries would be the wiser.

My heart skips a beat at the thought. One leg twitches, as though urging me to make a run for it.

But I can't. I'm no deserter. As much as I want to run to my husband and missing son, as much as I want to protect the child growing inside of me, I can't leave.

I'm a valkyrie and this is my battle. This isn't just about winning my own freedom. It's about earning the freedom of valkyries everywhere. About honoring the fallen, the ones who've given their lives for this cause. Fleeing would dishonor them.

I need to see this to the finish.

Crack!

The ground splits again. In the distance, I hear humans crying out. Another reason to keep fighting. This is a battle that should've never found its way here. It needs to stop before the planet is destroyed.

I take a deep breath and ready my sword, then I run toward the chaos. My wings spread out and flap, lifting me into the air. I aim the blade into a valkyrie on the other side, making her fall to the ground.

The valkyrie she was fighting nods a thank you before spinning around and battling another.

I make my way to another and swing my sword. This time, the

valkyrie sees it coming and blocks my attack. I swing again, she blocks. Then she swings, and I block.

It goes on until she pins me against a tall tree and presses the tip of her blade against my neck. "Last chance to choose the right side!"

I squirm, but can't get away. "I have chosen the right side!"

She digs her sword into my flesh. Warm liquid oozes down, and I feel essence leave me.

This can't be it. It can't.

The other valkyrie's eyes widen. She gasps. Blood drips from her mouth. Her sword falls to the ground.

I gasp, confused and trying to inhale.

She clutches her chest before falling.

Behind her floats my mother, her sword dripping with blood. She wipes it across her shirt. "That was close!"

I just struggle to breathe. Can't find words. I almost died, but my mother saved me. My mother.

It hardly seems possible.

She comes closer. "Take some essence."

Before I can respond, she opens her mouth and the mist twists out of her mouth toward me. The silkiness weaves its way down my throat. Energy runs through me in waves. The wound in my neck closes.

I find my voice. "Thanks."

"You think I'd let you die?"

Truth is, I don't know what to think about her or her motives. Why would I?

"We'd better get back to it." She nods toward the fighting valkyries.

"How are we going to beat Odin?" I pull sticky hair from my face.

She wipes something from my neck. "Who says we have to?"

"What?"

"He's facing off with warriors from each side. Interrogating everyone. It doesn't appear he's decided yet."

I look over at him. He *is* talking with the valkyrie he's sword fighting with. "You're right." I let it sink in. "You really think he'd choose the opposition?"

My mother steps closer. "I heard a rumor that he and the others disappeared because they grew tired of the politics."

"They retreated? That can't be."

She shakes her head. "No, they didn't. From the sounds of it, they wanted a break from all the stress and annoyance. They've been discussing what to do over drinks and massages."

"For more than fifty years?"

"Fifty years is barely a blink for the likes of such ancients."

My mind spins as I take it all in. "Could Odin possibly think we're right? Would the others agree?"

"Sounds like they're as sick of everything as we are."

"Have you actually talked with him?"

"Not yet. Come on, we need to get back to it." She heads back toward the fighting.

I follow her, trying to decide if I believe Odin could potentially agree with us. Even if he did, there would be eleven others to convince, all of whom are equal to him in strength.

My mother and I stick together, fighting against our own kind. We eventually make our way to my father, then the three of us battle as one.

Eventually, we make it to Odin.

I want to flee. My mother grabs my arm. She must sense my apprehension.

My parents both salute Odin. Awkwardly, so do I. I've never been so close to him or any of the other top leaders. The power exuding from him knocks the wind from my lungs.

"Good work, soldiers." Odin puts his sword away and he relaxes.

I stare at him, then at my parents. If I could find my voice, I'd demand to know what's going on.

Nothing makes sense.

Odin adjusts his shirt. "I think we're ready to take this back to Valhalla."

Blood drains from my body. Back to Valhalla?

The mighty leader raises his arms high and snaps his finger.

Everything spins around me.

CHAPTER THIRTY-ONE

itan

I freeze in place and look around the demolished street. "Do you feel that?"

Toby nods. "Something's different."

"Maybe Alaska is close." *Please let him be close.* We've been searching for days, despite the earthquakes and flooding.

Eveline frowns. "It feels like the valkyries. Something drastic has happened."

Soleil.

Everything within me screams to run back to the battleground. "What happened?"

Eveline shakes her head. "I have no idea."

"A fine lot of help you are," I mutter.

"I could run a spell."

"Sorry for snapping. It isn't your fault. I hate having my family spread all over the place. I don't know where any of them are!"

"We're getting closer to Alaska."

"Unless he's moved since your last locator spell." I pull on my hair.

Gessilyn comes over. "What I feel is a *lack* of valkyries. Their energy is different from the rest of us. It went from strong to practically nonexistent."

I close my eyes. Nonexistent means they've all gone to Valhalla —the ones who haven't died, that is.

Gessilyn rests a hand on my shoulder. "Let's find Alaska."

"Unless they took him back to Valhalla."

"Eveline's right. We're close."

"You should run the spell again."

I look around at the destruction. The suburb has been destroyed. Buildings have crumbled, street signs are spread across the road, cars are on top of each other, crushed. If Alaska was here during the earthquakes and flooding, could he have survived? Sure, he stood up against the hunters, but would he know what to do in the face of natural disasters?

Eveline clears her throat. "I think we should keep going. We're so close."

Crack!

I hold my breath, expecting another earthquake. But instead of the ground shaking, the sky turns orange. Bright orange. Then black.

Screams sound. I can't tell who is yelling. Could be humans, could be some of our own.

I shake. Can't help it. I'm so cold. Can't see anything. People are still screaming.

The sky lights up again. I can see.

Valkyries are falling from the sky. Not falling. Flying. Swords in hands.

My pulse drums in my ears. I scan the crowd for Soleil, but from this distance, they all look the same. She could be any one of them, or none of them.

Soleil could be back in Valhalla, in the torture yards she's talked about so many times.

I have a feeling I'm about to find out. Was our time together all we'll ever get? Or will we get to live our dream? And what about Alaska? Our other child?

Valkyries land around with grace, like they hadn't just come down from the sky.

Clenching my fists, I study each face. Though similar to her, none is her.

I can't breathe.

Maybe she came down somewhere else. Near the mansion. Or in Australia. Egypt. She loves Egypt. *Please be in Egypt.*

Toby nudges me. Nods his head toward my back. Is that hope in his eyes?

I spin around.

Soleil.

Is that really her? I rub my eyes.

Still there. Walking toward us. Her expression lights up when our gazes lock.

We both burst into a run at the same time. I nearly knock someone over as I race to the love of my life. She's alive. Here on Earth. Not in a torture yard.

We slam into each other. I wrap my arms around her. Cling to her. Breathe her in. She smells like fresh mountain air.

I kiss her desperately. Never wanting to let her go again. Silently pleading that this is hello and not goodbye. How has Odin's appearance changed everything? Did the valkyries defeat him? Bow to his authority? Is Soleil free or still owned by Valhalla?

None of those questions, or a thousand more racing through my mind, reach my mouth. She's in my arms, and for the moment, that's the only thing that matters.

Then she pulls back. "I'm free."

I blink a few times. "You are?"

She nods. "We won. It's all over."

Seems too good to be true. I wait for her to drop the bad news.

"Where's Alaska? Did you find him?"

I look down and shake my head. "Not yet. Eveline and Gessilyn say we're close, though."

Soleil grabs my hand. "Let's find him. I'll explain everything along the way."

"What's going on with the valkyries coming from the sky? Are they free too?"

"We're all free. Most want to remain soldiers, but it's all voluntary. They can take breaks whenever they need to as long as they transfer their targets to someone else."

We reach the others, and everyone envelops Soleil in warm embraces. I step back and try to take in the news.

She's free. Really and truly.

Eveline comes over. "I re-ran the spell. Alaska is close. Really close."

"Where?" I glance around.

"Maybe in one of these buildings, or just beyond. I wish these things were a little more precise."

I swallow. "But the fact that you found him means he's alive, right?"

She nods. "It was a quick find. Strong signal."

Relief washes through me. "Lead the way!"

Eveline weaves through the crowd.

We follow her, and I grab Soleil. "Alaska's over there."

Her eyes widen. We race to catch up with Eveline.

As we near the first building, I call out to my son. "Alaska!"

Soleil cups her mouth. "Alaska!"

Others call out for him.

"Mom... Dad..."

I skid to a stop and turn to Soleil. "Did you hear that?"

She nods.

We both race for the building. Half the walls have crumbled to the ground. The roof is cracked and diagonal, partially on the ground and partially attached.

My heart skips a beat. He's in there? I pull away from Soleil's hold and leap over debris and crawl in through a shattered window. I scrape my arm, and blood drips down. "Alaska!"

"Dad..."

He sounds so weak, it breaks my heart.

"I'm coming! Where are you?"

Soleil jumps through the same broken window. She lands without so much as a mark. "Alaska!"

My wound throbs.

"Mom..." His voice comes from the left.

Soleil and I both race in that direction, her more gracefully than me. She easily jumps over broken furniture and crumbled walls.

Alaska is still calling out to us. His voice is getting louder. Closer.

We come to a dead end. There's a staircase, but it's completely blocked. No way to get around it. Our son isn't anywhere in sight.

"Alaska!" I flip over a table and some boards.

"Here..."

Soleil and I tear through the debris, following his voice.

"Over here!" She waves me toward her.

I race over, stumbling.

"He's under this door! Help me lift it."

A steel door is sprawled out over a crushed table. It's jammed underneath a fallen wall and one corner is sticking out through a busted window.

I kneel and grab the corner Soleil is lifting. Even with both of us pulling, the door barely budges.

"Hey, Alaska," I grunt. "If you're under there, push the door up. We need your help!"

"I'll try."

"You can do it," Soleil urges.

Sweat drips into my eyes as I strain. "We're going to have to try something else."

Footsteps sound behind. Our friends race over and help us. Even with a dozen of us, the door barely budges.

I turn to Soleil. "Drink my essence."

She shakes her head.

"You have to! It'll make you stronger. It isn't helping me."

Eveline steps over. "Take mine, then."

Soleil shakes her head again. "I'm not taking anyone's essence after everything we've been through. Everything my kind has put us all through."

"Okay. Have it your way. Step back." Eveline stares at the door. "You leave me no choice. I'll have to use magic to explode it."

"Explode it?" Soleil jumps up. "Are you crazy? You could hurt him!"

"He has to get out one way or another, right?"

Soleil's brows draw together. "Fine. I'll take your essence."

Eveline smirks, like this was her plan.

Soleil doesn't seem to notice. She closes her eyes and opens her mouth. Her wings burst out and her eyes glow bright green under her lids. Eveline's eyes close and mist twists out of her mouth and makes its way into Soleil's.

Almost as soon as it starts, it stops. Soleil opens her eyes and the electric green nearly lights up the dim room. "On three, we lift!" We gather around the door again and each take hold of it. "One. Two. Three!"

I pull, expecting it to resist like before. Instead, the door flies up as if it were only a feather, and it sails through the air. Some of the werewolves scatter out of the way before it crashes on top of them.

It takes me a moment to realize I'm actually looking at Alaska. He looks even older than before. If I didn't know better, I'd think he was old enough to legally drink alcohol.

Soleil falls to her knees and embraces him. I kneel and wrap my arms around both of them, never wanting to let go.

But the walls around us shake. Another earthquake? Is the valkyrie war not over, after all?

"Run!" someone yells.

I pull Soleil and Alaska up, then race for the window we came in through. Everyone else piles out after us.

No sooner does the last person escape when what's left of the building crashes down on where we all just stood. I cling to my family, hardly able to believe how close we made it.

CHAPTER THIRTY-TWO

Soleil

Titan hands me a rainbow-colored drink in a glass with a little umbrella and sits next to me. He glances over at Alaska building a sandcastle with Cairo, who was born a month after the civil war ended. We decided to give our daughter the name of a place, like we had with our son.

Nobody would ever guess by looking at them that they're actually less than a year apart in age. Alaska looks about twenty, and we're lucky he didn't age past that based on the story he told us about drinking five valkyries dry the day he escaped captivity. It turns out that he can trick people, and without realizing it, he'd made the valkyries think he was Odin. Our best guess is that he made them see their worst fear, but we don't know for sure as we don't understand his powers fully yet. They're similar to both Titan's and mine, but different.

From there, he made his way to the building where we eventually found him. An earthquake trapped him beneath the door, nearly crushing him, but actually protecting him from getting hurt.

"Are you going to drink that?" Titan teases.

I sip the delicious beverage and arch a brow. "You got more unicorn horn flakes?"

"Maybe." His eyes sparkle as he sips from his cup.

"Momma!" Cairo toddles over, holding a shell. "Look what I found!"

I set my glass on the tray between Titan and me then scoop her up. "It's beautiful."

She beams. "Can I keep it?"

"Of course."

"Hold it." She shoves it in my hand and climbs off the chair, toddling back over to her brother.

My phone rings.

Titan groans. "Tell me it isn't your parents."

My mother and father have been appointed the top valkyrie leaders here on Earth, and given how rocky the new Valhalla government has started, they've called me numerous times for help with one issue or another.

I pick up the phone and glance at the screen. "Nope. Just Eveline."

He breathes a sigh of relief. "Tell her to build a snowman for us."

I snicker as I accept the call. "Hey, Eveline. Isn't it pretty late over there?"

"A witch's work is never done, especially when she's learning from the high witch's family."

"True." I sip my drink. "Do you need my help with something?"

"Everyone has been asking me if you're going to have a birthday party for Alaska. Toby says you can have it at the mansion."

"I'm sure he wants one, but we'll host it. We have this entire beach to ourselves. It'll give you all a good excuse to get away from your wintery weather."

"It's not that bad. We haven't seen a single snowflake this year."

"Let me guess, all rain and wind."

"Actually, the werewolf kids were outside playing in the sun today."

I yawn. "You're not convincing me."

She laughs. "Okay, okay. So, party at your Australia home?"

"Nothing's written in stone yet. Alaska has been talking about wanting to explore another pyramid. He may want an Egyptian party."

"Let us know. I'm sure nobody will complain about going somewhere warmer."

"Ha! I knew it." I grin.

Titan gives me a sideways glance, obviously trying to figure out what we're discussing.

"Oh! One more thing," Eveline says as we're about to end the call.

"What's that?"

"Toby and Victoria wanted me to remind you that your room is always there for you at the mansion."

"Tell them we'll be there in the spring. When it's warmed up a bit."

"Okay. Can't say he won't be disappointed, though."

We laugh, then say our goodbyes.

Titan leans closer. "Planning a party?"

"They're trying to talk us into having Alaska's birthday at the mansion, but I can't see leaving the warmth." I swing my legs over and bury my toes in the warm sand.

He cups my chin and brushes his lips across mine. "As long as we're together and don't have to worry about Valhalla calling you back, I don't care where we are."

"Mmm. Me neither, actually. And with my parents running things here, we don't have anything to worry about."

"Momma! Daddy!" Cairo waves us over.

"See the sandcastle we built!" Alaska beams like the youngster he is.

Titan slides his fingers through mine as we join our kids.

Alaska's forehead wrinkles when he looks at me.

"Are you okay?" I ask.

He glances at my stomach. "Another sister?"

Titan and I exchange surprised looks.

I turn to Alaska. "It would appear so."

"Yay!" Cairo jumps up and down, sending sand in all directions.

Alaska grins. "I've got Grandma's gift."

"You have a lot of gifts." Titan pats him on the back, then turns to me. "And it looks like we might have as many kids as my parents."

His comment knocks the wind from my lungs.

He laughs. "I'm only teasing."

My phone rings. I glance at the screen. It's one of Valhalla's newly-appointed leaders.

I throw my phone into the ocean and turn back to my loved ones. "Let's celebrate our growing family."

WHAT'S NEXT?

(Spoilers ahead if you skipped to this part.) Now that Soleil's series is completed, you may be wondering what's next—especially since most of my paranormal series are connected! Valhalla's Curse was spun off from the Curse of the Moon series (Toby and Victoria's story) and that was spun off from the Transformed series (the vampire king and queen's tale).

Will there be more? Or is this the end of the story world and characters we've grown to love? It might be hard to tell since I didn't leave any threads hanging...

Or did I? Okay, I didn't. But I did leave some clues as to what's coming next. Stop and think for a moment and see if you can guess who might be next. Is there someone who you really want to know more about? A character who seems like they have some really interesting surprises in store?

If you're like most of my early readers, then your answer is probably Alaska, the boy who grew up too fast. Way too fast! And what about his powers? Nobody understands them yet, and it seems like they ought to be interesting as he grows and matures.

So, what's the plan? Alaska's series will begin either at the end of this year (2019) or in the early part of next year. Why so far away?

Because I have a mermaid trilogy planned for the middle of this year. (Probably in the spring or summer.) It's not related to anything else, but it's going to be a lot of fun, and I'm excited about it. He's a brooding guitarist looking to make a name for himself and she's a frustrated mermaid eager to leave her harsh watery world behind. When they meet, things are bound to turn more than a little awry—especially when their best friends intervene.

If you enjoy reading in other genres, you may be interested in some of my other works. Currently, I'm writing the next Alex Mercer thriller and also planning another Indigo Bay sweet romance. Plus, there's another project, but it's so up in the air, I can't really say much more than that right now.

To make sure you don't miss anything, be sure to sign up for my book updates:

http://stacyclaflin.com/newsletter/

Meanwhile, **if you haven't read the books leading up to Soleil's series,** you should check them out. You'll likely enjoy them since you liked Valhalla's Curse enough to finish it...

MORE OF SOLEIL'S STORY WORLD

While you wait for *Silenced Valkyrie*, there are plenty more books to read set in this magical world. Do you want a standalone? Or do you want to see where we first met Soleil? Or one of the other characters? No matter what you'd like to read next, you're sure to find it in one of the twenty-four previous books!

If you want more of Soleil, read *Lost Wolf*, where we first meet her.

She's hiding a dark secret. It already killed her once.

Victoria can't wait to start college, but there's a hitch—she can't remember anything before arriving on campus. Her memories spark when she sees her ruggedly handsome math professor, but she senses something horrific. The shock on his face affirms her fears.

Toby is an alpha wolf who never thought he'd see his true love again— not after she died in his arms. Nothing could have prepared him for her walking into his class. But to his dismay, not only has she forgotten what happened, she doesn't even know who she is.

He's determined to do whatever it takes to restore what they've lost. Can Toby help Victoria recover her memories, or will he lose her forever?

Excerpt:

Attention, please," Professor Foley said and turned around.

Grace snapped her attention toward the front. I followed suit.

"Welcome," he continued.

I studied his profile. There was something familiar about him. My heart raced at the thought.

He continued speaking, focused on the other side of the group. I couldn't understand a word he said. The longer I stared at him, the more convinced I became that somehow I knew him. Or at least had seen him somewhere.

His hair was dark and thick, his skin tanned to perfection. He had stunning features and a gorgeous profile. It was hard to believe he was old enough to be a professor. He was younger by far than all the others I'd seen. A magazine cover would have been a more fitting place for him.

Professor Foley turned toward my side of the group. "And be sure to ask questions. That's what we're here..." His voice trailed off as our gazes met. His face paled and his eyes widened. His expression held something. Horror? Shock? Whatever it was, he continued staring at me.

I was frozen in place. My heart thundered in my chest, threatening to break through my ribcage. I knew him. Without a doubt, we had spent time together. I just couldn't remember any of it. My palms had grazed that stubble and my eyes had stared into those deep blue eyes. Even with the distance, I recalled that he often smelled of woodsy aftershave and soap.

Those around me whispered, bringing me back to the present.

Professor Foley cleared his throat and glanced around at the other students. "Excuse me. As I was saying, the faculty is here to help you. Just don't wait until the final hour."

"What was that?" Grace whispered.

My mouth gaped and I shook my head.

"You know him or something?"

"Shh," I snapped.

"Sorry." She scooted away.

My hands shook. I sat on them to get them to stop.

Foley stopped talking, and everyone paired off. Grace glanced at me, her expression pensive.

I nodded and tried to push the instructor out of my mind. But how could I? He was my only clue to my past. Part of me longed to run around the other students and throw my arms around him.

Grace came over. "I wasn't trying to bother you before."

"I know. Sorry. What are we supposed to do?"

"We're supposed to discuss…"

My gaze wandered back over to Professor Foley. He was speaking to a couple students and smiling. My chest constricted. Oh, that smile. It had taken my breath away countless times, though I couldn't remember a single one of them.

Read   Lost   Wolf!   Links   here: http://stacyclaflin.com/books/lost-wolf/

If you want a standalone…

Read *Sweet Desire*, which is Gessilyn's story:

Fate can only be avoided for so long. Gessilyn's time is up.

She has been living a quiet life pretending to be human for many years, but now she's a witch on the run. Claudia, her old rival, has found her—and she wants Gessilyn dead.

If she's to survive, Gessilyn must return to her roots and learn magic from a father she never knew. The power within her reveals itself to be stronger than anyone has ever seen, and Gessilyn finds herself more a risk to herself than anyone else is until she can learn to control it.

While needing to focus on all she has to learn, Gessilyn finds herself increasingly drawn to Killian, the handsome loner in her father's coven. She tries to ignore her growing feelings, but they only intensify. Will she be able to hone her powers in time to defeat Claudia, or will Killian distract her and become her downfall?

Excerpt:

The moon's glow on my skin tingled. Then it intensified to a near-burn. It shone full and bright. I gritted my teeth and ignored the discomfort. My pain indicated something more ominous coming.

Cawing from a murder of crows disrupted the quiet of the night. I shuddered at the irony of the group's name because they announced ominous things to come. They circled the outline of the moon. It gave them an eerie glow. They grew louder.

"Is this a warning for me?"

Silence.

Several woodland creatures scurried away.

Goosebumps formed on my arms and neck. I swept my long hair to the side and twisted it around my manicured nails. The moonlight made it seem especially blonde.

I took a deep breath and ran a finger along the skirt of my dress. "Do you have a message for me?"

The black scavengers flew erratically, completely blocking my view of the moon. Their cawing sounded more like screams. I wanted to cover my ears but refused myself the comfort. The noise became deafening.

I squatted to the ground, refusing to leave. I needed to figure out their message.

The birds dispersed and disappeared from sight as quickly as they'd appeared.

Gasping for breath, I stood and steadied my shaking arms. My heart thundered in my chest. I was no closer to understanding the message, but I had ways of finding out.

Links here: http://stacyclaflin.com/books/sweet-desire-3/

Carter and Katya's Story

How did Carter find Katya? What's their love story, and all the danger surrounding it? Find out in *Secret Jaguar*.

A cat has nine lives, but that doesn't mean she should forfeit one of them.

Katya Pelletier is the practical, no-nonsense twin. She loves life as much as her sister, she just doesn't seem able to enjoy it as much. While Alley is the life of the party and has boyfriends to spare, Katya can't seem to attract anyone's attention.

Until she meets Carter Jag.

Carter is the perfect male specimen. By all rights, he should be chasing after Alley. But to Katya's surprise—and confusion—he's only interested in her.

As their relationship progresses, something primal and passionate awakens in Katya. She's introduced to and immersed in a whole world she never knew existed. A paranormal world. A world of antiquated ideas and imminent danger. Katya is a jaguar shifter, and her former "family" has come to claim their prize—her.

Katya joins Carter and his supernatural allies in the fight of her life—a battle to free her from her former family and their outdated ways. But will their power and magic be enough to save her from the life of violence and servitude the jaguars are determined to force on her?

Read an excerpt and find links here: https://stacyclaflin.com/books/secret-jaguar/

If you want to start at the very beginning...

Deception is my first book and also where it all started—and also where we first meet Marguerite. (Although she doesn't know she's Marguerite yet!) You can read *Deception*—my first published novel—for free in ebook form...

What if your whole life was a lie?

Alexis Ferguson wasn't blessed with the perfect body, but the ambitious overachiever has used her book smarts to get her where she is today. It's too bad that everything she knows is wrong.

After meeting a gorgeous stranger on a blind date, Alexis feels like she's known him her entire life. Suddenly, dark long-forgotten memories swirl in her mind. She realizes she's powerful, stunningly beautiful, and marked for death.

As she faces the one who ordered her execution years ago, Alexis must learn her strange new powers and trust in unlikely allies to keep herself alive.

Excerpt:

As I stood in the woods, the hair on my arms and neck stood up, and I knew I was being watched. Here it was—the moment of truth. It was of little comfort to know that at least I wasn't going to get mauled to death.

I listened for anything unusual or any sound that would give me a clue as to where the animal or person might be. Nothing seemed out of place.

I wanted to run up a tree and hide, but I had to stand exposed in the middle of the stupid clearing and wait for my predator to show itself or until I could track it down.

My heart raced. Was Clara messing with me? I swallowed and looked for someone hiding in the woods. When I had made three-quarters of a turn, I felt that I had reached the direction that I needed to focus on. My skin was crawling with the sensation of being watched. I wanted to scream from both frustration and fear.

I looked around. It felt like I was staring at one of those pictures where you're supposed to see a hidden scene if you let yourself go cross-eyed. I never could find those hidden scenes, but hoped this would be different.

My nerves were shot and I didn't feel like putting up a fight. I wanted to crawl into bed, but my life might be on the line, so that was clearly not an option.

Finally, I thought I saw something. It looked somewhat like a head, hiding and blending in between some bushes. I took a deep breath and braced myself. I thought my mind might be playing tricks on me, but I was pretty certain I was looking at the head of whomever was causing all the distress on my senses.

I heard a light rustle, and nearly jumped and ran off. My heart was racing, and it was so loud I was sure he could hear it too. I turned my attention back to the one watching me. I couldn't tell if I was truly in danger, or if he was just having fun scaring me. At least it couldn't read my mind.

I crouched down a little, gaining some confidence. I couldn't believe it when I started walking toward him. In my mind, I screamed at my legs to stop, but they refused to obey. I continued to walk directly toward him, as though it was the prey, and I was the predator.

When I had gone about twenty yards, I could see him smile. That infuriated me, and I wanted to attack the prideful thing.

"Show yourself!" I commanded with more confidence than I actually felt.

Read **Deception** **for** **free.** Link here: http://stacyclaflin.com/books/deception

OTHER BOOKS BY STACY CLAFLIN

If you enjoy reading outside the romance genre, you may enjoy some of Stacy Claflin's other books, also. She's a *USA Today* bestselling author who writes about complex characters overcoming incredible odds. Whether it's her Gone saga of psychological thrillers, her various paranormal romance tales, or her romances, Stacy's three-dimensional characters shine through bringing an experience readers don't soon forget.

The Gone Saga

The Gone Trilogy: Gone, Held, Over

Dean's List

No Return

Alex Mercer Thrillers

Girl in Trouble

Turn Back Time

Little Lies

Against All Odds

Don't Forget Me

Curse of the Moon

Lost Wolf

Chosen Wolf

Hunted Wolf

Broken Wolf

Cursed Wolf

Secret Jaguar

Valhalla's Curse

Renegade Valkyrie

Pursued Valkyrie

Silenced Valkyrie

Vengeful Valkyrie

The Transformed Series

Main Series

Deception

Betrayal

Forgotten

Ascension

Duplicity

Sacrifice

Destroyed

Transcend

Entangled

Dauntless

Obscured

Partition

Standalones

Fallen

Silent Bite

Hidden Intentions

Saved by a Vampire

Sweet Desire

Short Story Collection

Tiny Bites

The Hunters

Seaside Surprises

Seaside Heartbeats

Seaside Dances

Seaside Kisses

Seaside Christmas

Bayside Wishes

Bayside Evenings

Bayside Promises

Bayside Destinies

Bayside Opposites

Bayside Chances

Standalones

Lies Never Sleep

Dex

Haunted

Fall into Romance

AUTHOR'S NOTE

Thanks so much for reading *Unleashed Valkyrie*. I hope you've enjoyed this series as much as I have. Soleil started off as spunky side character in my Curse of the Moon series, and I knew early on that she needed a story of her own. And now there's a character from this series who seems to be screaming for a series. Who? As mentioned in the "What's Next" section, it's Alaska! I'm excited to see where he takes us.

It's always fun to have a character inspire another series. One of my favorite parts of that is bringing in characters from previous books. It's like visiting old friends. Keep an eye out for future books! The best way to do that is to join my newsletter because I also send out new release alerts. You can also follow me on social media, Bookbub, and your favorite online retailer.

If you enjoyed this book, please consider leaving a review wherever you purchased it. Not only will your review help me to better understand what you like—so I can give you more of it!—but it will also help other readers find my work. Reviews can be short—just share your honest thoughts. That's it.

I've spent many hours writing, re-writing, and editing this work. I even put together a team who helped with the editing process. As it is impossible to find every single error, if you find any, please contact me through my website and let me know. Then I can fix them for future editions.

Thank you for your support! I really appreciate it—and you guys! Until next time...